THE EVENING OF BARTHOLOMEW JONES

JK George

JK George

ISBN: 9798396498600

Cover design by JK George

Printed in the United States of America

I dedicate this book to my wife, Wendy, without whose love and support during the past three years, it would have remained unwritten.

CONTENTS

Ch 1. Bart

Bart had booked a hotel near the airport. An early flight, an opportunity for quiet. He had just spent five days with his daughter, Sophie, her husband, Tom, three grandchildren whose birthdays he had forgotten or never knew, and Otis, a sixty-pound Boxer puppy. Upon entering their house in Maryland, Otis had greeted him with a standing face lick and clawed his arms into ads for pepperoni pizza. Later, after apologies and first aid, his three grandchildren joined Otis, and the foursome continued a daily crash and squeal throughout the house. For meals, well, one big trough would have sufficed. Five days was a long time.

As he walked to room 120, children dressed for bed shrieked from room 114 and spilled down the disappearing corridor. An abandoned room-service tray sat on the hall carpet, offering a dried piece of whole wheat toast and a wilted rose in a small white vase. Outside, cars circled the hotel, driving slowly, crunching the ice. He wondered why the desk clerk gave him two key cards.

Room 120 smelled slightly of disinfectant. The room displayed a tightly made queen size bed, a foot of exposed white sheet, two chairs, a desk, and a black expanse of TV. A small card said "Sonja" cleaned the room. Bart turned on the heat. He could still hear shouts from 114.

About ten minutes to ten the room phone rang. Bart's daughter, Sophie, wanted to know if he had made it safely to the hotel. With tongue in cheek, he told her that upon entering the hotel, he spent 20 minutes trapped in the hallway resisting some strange woman with long red hair who wanted to spend the night with him. She told him that she didn't want a relationship, just a night of continuous sex. Of course he refused, preferring to spend his evening reading Sir Philip Sidney.

Feigning seriousness Sophie said, "I would have made the same choice. There's nothing like a 16th century poet for a night's rest--or eternal rest for that matter. So how's the room?"

"Cold. White. I think they use it as an operating room when they're not renting it to travelers. The housekeeper's name, by the way, is Sonja. She left me a handwritten note. Extremely personal. I'm going to leave her ten bucks. Next time I stay here I should get notes from Maintenance and Security as well."

"Next time you'll have to stay longer with us. It meant a lot to the kids, Dad, and to Tom and me as well." She paused. "And, of course, there's Otis."

"Yeah, I would certainly come back for Otis. I can hear him now."

"No, you're hearing the kids. I've got to put them to bed, or I may kill them tomorrow. Love you, Dad. Get some sleep." The call ended.

Bart sat for a moment looking at the silent phone. Despite the banter and well-wishes, Sophie had changed. More the mother, less the daughter. Maybe she was right. Maybe she spoke a truth he did not want to hear. He didn't know. He wanted to go home.

Three months later.

American Flight 352 left Dulles just as the sun appeared and flew west into the darkness. On arrival in San Jose, Sophie would drive south another three hours to the coastal town of San Sebastian. She considered flying from San Jose to San Luis Obispo, the county seat, but the flight didn't leave San Jose until the next morning and the drive beat paying for a motel. Besides she needed time to think.

5'3" Sophie had a window seat. People wouldn't crawl

over her, and, assuming it worked, she would control the window shade. She thought of her family, her dad, and her brother, Nate, and she was annoyed at her brother. Here she was, flying across the country to check out their father, talk him into something. "I can't talk to him," said Nate. "He's died in place. Does nothing these days but stay in the house. Says he's tired."

Sophie looked at her novel. Airplane reading. Crap. She had managed to read one paragraph in the last half hour and didn't remember what it said. Finally she gave up, put the book away.

When Dad last visited, he was a bit older, but nothing different. Irreverent, obscene, outspoken. She still remembered the dinner conversation the last evening of Dad's visit and smiled in spite of herself. Dad had said his vet told him that Lily, his poodle, had some vaginal discharge and he should keep an eye on it. Dad said when he got home, he didn't have any idea where the thing was located and went on describing his search. Tom was embarrassed. The kids had loved it.

But he had seemed tired when we talked lately, and I do trust Nate and his judgment. Still it pisses me off that I get to be the heavy, the one who does the dirty work. And where is Nate? He's in Montreal. Business or so he says.

After picking up her rental car, Sophie drove south down Highway 101, thought about what she would say to her dad and in what shape she would find the house. Dark, with that alone smell? Newspapers piled up on the porch? No, Dad was a neat freak. The house would look fine. He hired everything done, though she bet he ate his meals cold from cans. How does she tell him he needs to get a life?

When Sophie arrived, the house looked as it always did —imposing, smooth grey stucco, manicured lawn, clean. The house had aged well. And Bart looked much like he had always looked: grey-black hair, dark eyes, an athlete gone somewhat to fat. Otherwise just an older version of the lawyer/ex-Marine she had grown up with.

Though tired from travel, Sophie knew that she would not sleep until she talked with her father, or at least began the talk. And "talked", not merely caught up. She could at least find out what he had not been doing over a glass of wine and have a serious conversation in the morning. She still wouldn't sleep, but by morning she might know what to say.

She should have known better. Bart put his arm around her shoulders. "So, what's up? You split from your husband or something?"

"No, I actually came to talk with you."

"With me? What have I done?"

"That's just it. My spies tell me you're not doing much of anything, except sitting in this house imitating a broccoli."

Bart frowned, "Your brother put you up to this?"

"Maybe. Is it true that you're turning into a green vegetable?"

"Not sure, never thought about it. I certainly haven't done much of late." Bart raised his eyebrows, sat back in his chair. "What do you two think I should be doing?"

"You could start by cleaning out Mom's closet. I know it's hard; we all miss her, I'll help you if you like." Sophie straightened the photos on the mantle, put them in the order she remembered.

"And then go out, see other people, run, ride your Harley—date maybe."

"Date—I think you're describing a peach half, I'm just a broccoli."

Sophie shook her head. "Seriously, Dad. We've been worried about you, and it's not just us. People haven't seen you since Mom died, you dropped out of your Rotary club, you don't

4

take classes anymore, you don't answer messages. Mom's been gone for over a year. What's up?"

"Not much I guess. Bart leaned his head back, looked away for a moment. Returning to Sophie, he said, "I don't know, haven't wanted to do anything. Certainly haven't wanted to be around people, listen to all their fucking problems. Spent my life doing that."

"So, what's next? Shall we schedule a grave-side ceremony now so there will be no conflicts?"

"Well, I've got an empty calendar." Bart paused. "No, no. I'll get it together. I've been tired. Just haven't wanted to do much."

Sophie was encouraged. Her dad had just said he didn't have it together and might change. "I'm going to make a suggestion. You won't like it at first and it's going to be tough for you to do—somewhat like getting up off the floor and continuing a fight."

"Oh God," said Bart, "here it comes. . .. Let me guess. You want me to see a shrink?"

"I want you to talk with a counselor, like I did when my friend, Joan died. And that's all you really do, you talk. And what you'll find is in talking, somewhat directed talking, you'll discover what's bothering you and then you'll deal with it. Sometimes just talking about things is all it takes. The only scary thing about it, the part that takes a really strong person, is going in the first place and admitting to yourself that you could use some help in solving a problem. Like when your clients came to you for help."

Bart crossed his arms and gave Sophie a thoughtful look. "Not sure I want to do that. Think I'd rather just go down to Sunny Oaks, the old folk's home in town, and sleep in a wheelchair with all the others. There'd be ten of us together, all the same, heads back, mouths open. A big baby-bird room."

Sophie groaned.

He leaned forward taking both chair arms in his hands, "I really don't like this idea.

"How about a compromise? Forget about counseling and move to some place full of active people your age. Not an old folk's home. Think of a senior resort with as many activities as you want or don't want."

Bart scowled. "Are you now my mother?

"How about at least taking a look. Would you do that for me? There's a great place near where Nate lives. You might be surprised. Could do wonders for your love life."

"Hmm. Want some more wine?"

Sophie shook her head, looked around the room. Finally, looking straight at her father, she said, "Dad, I've already arranged a visit to the Sycamores—that's the name of the senior campus near Nate."

Bart sighed, suppressed a smile.

Ch 2. The Sycamores

"This is really lovely, Dad. I'm amazed they could build this place and save all these giant valley oaks."

"Must be why they call this place 'The Sycamores,'" said Bart, glancing at his watch.

"No doubt. But it is lovely.   And look at that walkway covered with wisteria. Beautiful. They must have transplanted mature plants."

"I'm sure they've transplanted mature residents," said Bart. As they walked toward the lobby, Bart read the various directional signs: Care Unit, Memory Unit—euphemisms, he knew, for Hospital and Locked. He suspected an underground conveyor belt transported expired residents between the care unit and a local mortuary.

As they walked toward the reception area, Sophie said, "Just keep an open mind, Dad. It's not something you need to do today or tomorrow (or ever thought Bart), but it could work later—especially with me so far away and Nate constantly on the run."

On arrival, the director of the facility, Ms. Pangok, elegantly dressed in fitted emerald silk, received Bart and Sophie and guided them to her paneled office with its quiet gold carpeting and panoramic windows. She wore a light perfume with just a hint of fragrance. Jasmine perhaps.

Entranced, Bart said, "I wouldn't mind hanging here."

"We have 400 acres at the Sycamores," said Ms. Pangok, "plenty of space to roam and hike, but at the same time enough to insure privacy. We have our own security force, not that we really need one. Crime in this area almost isn't." Ms. Pangok swept her arm across the vista. "What you see from these windows all belongs to us."

"Too perfect," whispered Bart. "Reminds me of a TV mystery where homes and people systematically disappear.

Welcome to Hotel California."

Sophie put her arm on his leg. "Shhh, just listen."

"Maybe, he continued, "it's an Aryan enclave, no offense Ms. Pangok, where all the elites have escaped from the metro."

"Be quiet. She'll hear you."

"At the moment we have a three-year waiting list—longer if you have a particular apartment in mind. So after the tour, if you like what you see, I would urge you to move quickly. Also, please be aware that you must pass a physical before you can become a resident. Although we provide medical care, we primarily focus on living."

"Yeah." said Bart under his breath, "Livin' the dream in the Memory Unit."

The apartments came in three sizes and most gave onto small enclosed gardens. Geraniums were popular—red, white, pink—all nearly unkillable in the mild California climate. Depending on availability and price, a resident had a choice of a studio, or a one- or two-bedroom apartment. All but the studio had one and a half baths. Since the Sycamores provided dining both in their restaurant or en suite, all sported a kitchen the size of a small coat closet but sufficient to accommodate a toaster, coffee maker, and mini fridge.

"Good," said Sophie, "a place to keep milk and fresh fruit."

"A place to keep my gin cold," said Bart, "or maybe Akvavit if I have Norwegian guests. But right now I'd settle for lunch."

They were then led to the facility dining room where the Sycamores Women's Club was presenting "Women Who Love Too Much" by Adelia Gorda. Fat, and wearing a rustling silk dress at least a size too small, Ms. Gorda jiggled as she moved.

Sophie frowned, "What a lecture to show a prospective resident."

Bart said, "She should retitle this: 'How Not to Suffocate

Your Date.' She could begin the lecture with an admonition: 'From the outset ladies, you should not use the praying mantis as a relationship guide.'"

"I'm sure, Dad, they have lectures on all sorts of subjects. If you noticed, there were only about 10 people present."

Later, they were shown to the library where an intense group listened to a woman shouting "B-3" and "A-5" and "D-1". No playfulness here. This stuff was serious.

"There's a lot of people here, but none of them are male. Probably all the men have suffocated."

"Stop", said Sophie."

"Well, except for the 'Loving Too Much' lecture, most residents I have seen are, in fact, alive, but shaky and uncertain of walk. And they all look alike, grey hair, tidy, neatly dressed in blue and rose pastels. Not a slob among the group."

Sophie said, "The ones that aren't tidy probably stay in their rooms and take advantage of the men who live here."

"And then they smother them, that's why you don't see any. You know it's almost noon."

Sophie jerked his arm, "Come on Dad, give it a chance. It beats the baby-bird room."

Ms. Pangok, rejoining the tour, interrupted their private conversation, "Everyone has something here for them, and the discussions keep minds engaged and active." Ms. Pangok then led a walking tour of the grounds and showed Bart several sizes of apartments, none furnished at Walmart. Covered cement walkways connected the various buildings and led through flowers and greenery. In several areas, gardeners replanted with fresh flowers and trimmed others. Residents sat on the occasional walkway benches, enjoying the smell of orange blossoms from the trees at the end of the facility.

Sophie said, "This is lovely. I could sit out here all afternoon. "

Bart said, "I'm starving." And, after loving women and Bingo, and at the invitation of Ms. Pangok, Bart and Sophie joined the residents for lunch. Bart wondered if the food was pre-chewed. It looked and smelled quite good, although no one appeared to be eating much of it.

They were seated at a table for eight. While Sophie answered questions from the women at the table—kids, husband, place of residence, &c.—Bart talked with Stan, his lunchmate, the only other male at the table. "After a while does the food all taste the same?"

Stan laughed. "Don't know. No one stays here long enough to get tired of it."

"Seriously?"

"No, just kidding. People travel, go to restaurants, and, of course, get sick and die. But, you know, everything's taken care of. Aside from paying your initial investment and monthly rent, you don't have to worry about a thing."

"So," said Bart, "I realize you can checkout—that is, die, but can you ever leave?"

"You probably wouldn't want to. If you did, you would lose your investment. And the investment is high. You're talking about a front-end cost starting at around a million. Most people sell their homes to raise the money for the investment. And the investment is not refundable. So, yes, you can check out, but really you can't leave unless you're totally bucks up. I mean, you can leave, but if you do, you may leave broke."

"And what do you do when you're not out and about?" And are there any men here?"

"Well, there's all sorts of planned activities—political discussions, travel films, speakers on various subjects, trips to local museums and performances. No sporting events to speak of. But you live your life as you always have, except no demands are made on you. You make your investment; pay your rent, and

Mother Sycamore takes care of you until you go out feet first."

"So, you're kept. God's waiting room."

"You're in God's waiting room wherever you are at our age —or preparing for a descent into the fire."

"And the men?"

"Married couples. But as you know, women live longer than men. We're definitely a minority. But that's not all bad."

"I suppose not, unless you're gay."

"I hadn't thought about it that way. But if you're hetero, and assuming that kind of thing still matters to you, there's plenty to choose from."

"So what did you do on the outside?" said Bart.

"I created computer programs to predict human behavior —both challenging and mentally demanding. I don't do much these days. I grow and photograph vegetables. You can have your own garden area if you want one."

While Bart and Stan talked, Sophie went off with the women she had met for a private tour. Told Bart she would meet him at reception. When she got there, Bart was checking stocks on his phone.

"So, how did it go, Dad?"

"It came and went. More old ladies than I thought existed."

"Isn't that a good thing?"

"What? Fungible old women? Think I'd rather go home and hustle Mrs. Higgins, my neighbor. At least she's ten years younger. The price would be right, and I don't think I would suffocate. Besides, I can't take Lily. No dogs."

"OK. Be negative. But keep it in mind. If Mrs. Higgins doesn't pan out, when you're 105 and semi-vegetable, you might discover some nuggets here that could interest you. You have to admit, the place is nice."

"It's exquisite, every amenity your heart could desire. And I did like Stan. But it scares me to death, not so much the place, but the surrender, the uselessness of life here, the bingo and the silly lectures. Stan designed computer models of human behavior. Now he now spends his time taking pictures of carrots and sits out on the ice floe waiting for the polar bear."

"And you're doing what at home?"

Bart ignored her. "Age doesn't limit what you can contribute. Older people can contribute if they want. They can write, they can design computer models, they can advise, they can reinvent themselves and lead new lives. Yes, the place is nice. It's well-appointed, first class. The landscaping with its flowers and trees paints the perfect picture and carries the smells of summer. All sorts of elegance here for people with money who have lost their usefulness and wait to die. But I'm sorry, Sophie. I'm not ready for the ice floe. Let's get out of here."

"How about counseling? Would you consider that?"

Bart felt his face flush but stopped from saying anything he'd regret. "Well, I think I would prefer counseling to an old folk's home. Maybe I should consider euthanasia and disposal."

"I think I might assist you after this morning."

He didn't need some shrink to tell him to get off his butt. He could do that on his own, though he knew he probably wouldn't. He had done nothing for the last two years but eat, sleep and watch TV. Sophie had flown 3000 miles to help him and now stood waiting, looking up at him as only a daughter can. And, after several moments she began to get tears in her eyes. Bart was strong, but not that strong. He took her hand. "I'll make you a deal. I'll go to counseling for a session or two at your expense, and we'll see how it works. You and Nate forget about care facilities, senior resorts, whatever you want to call them, for ten years--earlier if I'm completely nuts and think I'm Louis the 16th married to an Austrian princess. If I stay in counseling after a couple of sessions, I'll pay the freight. But I can stop at any time after the two sessions without your future mention of counseling or senior resorts. And, as a sweetener to the deal, I will shorten the ten-year period by two years if you can get Nate to pay for the shrink sessions. My best offer. What do you say?"

"How about four sessions?"

One month. He could do anything for one month. "Deal."

Ch 3. Children

Bach. Prelude and Fugue. Ringtone. In her purse. Where was her purse? Sophie raced upstairs. Found her purse. Found her phone. "Nathaniel Jones," said the screen. Nate, her brother. Sophie had returned from California only yesterday, and after reconnecting with her office, and after assisting her four children, really three children and a husband, Sophie had yet to unpack.

"So where are you? Still in Montreal?"

"Right now, I'm in DC, at the airport. I've an appointment tomorrow at 2:00, so thought I would come bother you if you'll have me, get the skinny on Dad."

"I don't know, Nate. I was really thinking of cleaning out my underwear drawer. Don't' want to leave things in a bunch." Sophie paused. Hearing no response she said, "Sure, come on out. I've been gone for a week. You can help me clean up. Lots of laundry. In the meantime, think of some expensive restaurant you'd like to take us to."

Having made the trip upstairs, Sophie took the clean clothes from her suitcase and began putting them away, keeping an eye out for her cat who would nest in the closet if he could get away with it, and tossed her dirty clothes into an already overflowing hamper.

Nate arrived about two hours later. Despite Sophie's annoyance at being manipulated by Nate—after all he lived 90 miles from Dad—she was glad to see him. As it turned out he had not been in Montreal but in Quebec City attending a "conference" at the Chateau Frontenac, the city's five-star hotel. He said he stayed there because there was a Starbucks on the street level.

Nate Jones was hard to dislike and had the boyish helplessness and gullibility that made every mother want to take care of him. Dark brown hair and eyes, a disarming smile,

6'3", he could pass for a pro quarterback. A two-day beard, his usual attire, complemented the package.

After a hug, Nate got right to the point. "So how was Dad?" Is he still running a senior brothel out of the two back bedrooms?"

"No, his stable currently is empty. The two remaining ladies died last week. 'Unstable' you might say."

"That's a shame. The youngest was only 95. Seriously, how was Dad? What did you find?"

Sophie thought about her visit. What had she seen? Stopping the banter, she looked at Nate. "Same Dad, different Dad. He didn't want to do much. Tired. Seemed mentally tired. I did manage to get him outside a couple of days and talk about things. And I got him to consider counseling. How that's going to work out, I have no idea. He's agreed to four sessions provided we make no mention to him of retirement homes for the next ten years, or unless he goes looneytoons. He can quit after the four sessions assuming he goes at all. I did tell him you agreed to pay for the counseling sessions, so you should expect to hear from him."

There was silence—delicious silence thought Sophie. She was really being an ass and she knew it.

"Really? You're joking."

"No, not joking. My airfare cost $700. Your turn in the barrel."

"And if he's still stationary after $700?"

"Well, then we can talk about it," said Sophie open-eyed and smiling. She was enjoying this conversation. "Maybe he'll die in the meantime and you won't have to pay."

"Right. Maybe I'll marry Jennifer Lopez. OK, I can do $700. But I'm not sure I can do Dad. He listens to you; he doesn't listen to me."

"He doesn't have to listen to you. You just need to pay his shrink bill. And who knows? It may be a one-shot deal, and then you can pay me the balance."

"OK, fine, whatever. Putting finances aside for the moment, sweet sister, what did you find? Is he going out at all? Doing anything? Visitors?"

"Not that I could tell. Neighbor lady to the north brings him food occasionally. Mrs. Higgins. You ever meet her?"

"No. There was no house there when I lived at home. Dad interested?"

"Don't think so. Of course he wouldn't talk to me about that. Might talk to you. She's an interesting person, up, cheerleader type."

"Sexy?"

"Maybe, if sixties is your thing. And big. Big, not fat. Pretty face, but she must be at least 5'11". Broad shouldered. Maybe played sports in college—water polo or softball. She definitely would start Dad's engine, but she's married. Don't think he'll get the chance. I'd love it if he were interested and be the dirty old man I always thought he'd be. You know, hang in the nursing home and pee in the potted plants. As I said, I did get him to do some things when I was there, shopping, a few walks, and a bust of a visit to the Sycamores, the senior place I told you about. But really he didn't want to do anything except stay at home and go to bed at 9:00. It was sad."

"So what's the next step?"

"Counseling I hope."

"So tell me more about this neighbor, Mrs. Whatever."

"Mrs. Higgins. Well, as I told you, she's big, looks like a big jock. Married. Husband's some type of engineer. Dad thinks he could bore grass. Mrs. Higgins—don't know her first name— I think teaches piano. Can't tell you much more than that. Nice lady, though. What about your Mrs. Higgins, your flavor of the month?"

"None at present. Glass of water and a toothpick. Women just aren't interested in money, intelligence and charisma. Actually my work schedule doesn't fit my love life. As soon as I meet someone, I'm out and about, sometimes for weeks. By the time I get back, she's gone."

"Have you considered another approach? You are in control, you know."

"Like what?"

"Like find your optimum prospect, someone who's brilliant, like me for example. Maybe an adjunct professor with a Ph.D. Hire her. Have her work for one of your staff—one of your female staff. Of course, you'll have to behave yourself. You can't hit on her, you'll get sued. You'll need to be subtle, although I know subtilty's a difficult thing for a male."

"Have someone in mind?"

"Not offhand. Maybe Mrs. Higgins has a daughter. Seriously, there's a glut of marginally employed Ph.D.'s, especially in the humanities. Of course if a female Ph.D. threatens you... "

They went out for designer pizza—Nate, Sophie, her husband, Tom; their three children. Nate paid.

Ch 4. Psychiatry 101

About 10 minutes early for his appointment, Bart parked his big Ford F-250 in the rear of the building where he sat for a while and thought about just staying in the truck. It had a great sound system and thick leather seats. But at 1:25, he got out and began his trek to the front. He kept his head down, hoped no one saw him. When he reached the covered porch, he stopped. He did not want to go in.

The psychiatrist counseled his patients in a small grey Craftsman with white trim. Uneven sidewalks, a tidy green lawn, and big locust trees fronted the house. There was a hidden parking lot in the rear, hidden so that a patient could avoid having to park on the street and possibly be recognized.

However discrete the parking lot, the doctor's patients entered the house from the front. The doctor had intentionally designed entry and exit so that when one patient entered the front, another left from the back. Schedules were offset so that there was, hopefully, no overlap, no recognition.

Unless a patient arrived by foot, the patient still had to walk from the back parking lot to the front of the house. Then, once in front and exposed to the world, but not to a fellow patient, the incoming patient walked up a cement pathway to a covered porch, complete with suspended swing. On the porch, he or she reached an imposing blond door, a door out of time and much too modern for the Craftsman house.

Bart looked around. He could go back to the truck, drive home, explain to the kids why he didn't go. Tell them what? That he was not afraid, but didn't want to be embarrassed? Embarrassed? Embarrassed about what? He had spent his career solving problems for other people, and he didn't think he needed other people to solve his problems. Maybe he could just tell the kids he enjoyed the session and was looking forward to the next one. They might believe it. They might never know he hadn't gone at all. But his children trusted him, and with their mother gone, this wasn't the time to lose their trust.

Bart stood on the porch. Thought for a second about the Lady and the Tiger, a story he remembered where the knight, or whatever he was, must choose between two closed doors. Behind one stood a lady he would be forced to marry; behind door number two stood a tiger and death.

This was stupid. Talking to a shrink was not death by tiger. But he was out in front like a billboard for all to see. He either should leave or go in. Seconds later a jogger appeared, running toward him in the distance. Bart opened the door and went in. Went into the small living room of the old house, now the waiting room of Dr. Anthony James, M.D., Doctor of Psychiatry.

Dr. James had furnished the room with Danish modern furniture upholstered in light blue. A "calming" color, Bart had learned. Pink would have done the same thing but had other meanings. James' furniture smelled new, the scent of the house older. Vague, faint, a smell of a past time when working men built houses by hand. Craftsman style but before the factory-made Craftsman houses. Lots of built-ins, glass, dark woods, all fit into 1500 square feet. Old vs. new sharing the same space.

After a short wait, a blond shaggy-haired man, probably in his early 30s, came into the waiting room and greeted Bart. He wore khaki pants, a tight black T-shirt, and sandals with black dress socks. "Hi," he said. "I'm Anthony James."

His youth and unprofessional appearance surprised Bart. James did not look like a shrink, or at least what Bart thought a shrink should look like. As they walked into the office, Dr. James pulled the patient's beige chair alongside his own, a large blue inflated ball. Responding to Bart's look, Dr. James said, "Keeps me fit while I'm sitting." Bart smiled. "Got it."

Side by side, Bart thought, apparently the good doctor wants to be with me and not against me. Time will tell. Moving the chair back opposite Dr. James, Bart sat down. He felt like a senior partner in the room with a new associate.

"You must have fun with your name," said Bart. "Anthony James, James Anthony. Probably helps you when you travel under cover."

"It has been fun. You'd be amazed how many bright people cannot read 'Last Name, First Name, Middle Initial'. I've sat through countless roll calls where some professor called 25 names without error and then called 'James Anthony.' At first I corrected. Later, I confess, I just raised my hand and said my name wasn't called. Just an unproductive form of getting even. Hopefully, I've matured."

Bart nodded, continued the interview. "So, Dr. Anthony, what's your background?"

Ignoring Bart, the doctor said, "I went to Sac State on a football scholarship. The big schools said I was too small to play Division 1 football. At Sac State I played linebacker, made all-league twice until I got injured.

"As an undergraduate, I majored in psychology then went to med school at UCSF. Interned for one year in Colorado followed by a three-year residency in psychiatry where I assessed and treated patients. Came back to the Central Coast three years ago and opened a practice. I like therapy. I believe it really helps people."

"Why'd you bother with med school? You don't need med school to practice oral therapy. You could be a porn star and practice oral therapy."

Bart examined the face of Dr. James, waited for a response. James paused, did not avoid Bart's gaze. "I'll have to think about that one." He stared at Bart for a moment and then in a confident voice said, "You do need training to become a psychologist. But as an M.D., I have a full range of treatment options. I can work in oral therapy--we call it talk therapy--which I think does the most good, and I can prescribe medication if needed, although I prefer not to. Also, should I tire of private practice, as a psychiatrist I am qualified to work for the local prison or the state mental hospital. Good pay; limited hours. That's why you'll find an unusual number of therapists in this county are psychiatrists.

Dr. James looked up at the clock on the wall. "My turn. I'd like to ask you a few questions before we run out of time.

"How do you feel about coming here? Sitting in front of a psychiatrist 30 years your junior?"

"Time will tell, I guess. You have an impressive background and appear well-trained. And I suppose people are people although I'm not sure someone in their 30s sees things through a sixty's lens."

"Assuming people are people and my training has embraced age differences, what do you expect to get out of these sessions?"

Bart shrugged, crossed his arms in front of his chest, then realizing what he had done, moved his arms onto his legs "I don't know. Maybe nothing. Maybe just calm down my daughter who thinks my death is imminent."

"Is it?"

"I'm not sure," said Bart. "I may already be dead."

"So how does that feel?" said the doctor. "Dead, I mean."

"Well, things go on, but Mary—Mary was my wife—Mary's not here. It's me and my dog, Lily. I look after the dog, change the sheets on my bed from time to time. There's not much else. Empty house, empty bed. Sometimes I watch Jeopardy."

"You watch TV?"

"Yeah, I guess, sometimes. . . . I sleep a lot." He slowly rocked back and forth in his chair.

"OK, so, other than satisfying your daughter, what might you want to get out of these sessions."

"Maybe satisfy my son, Nate as well. I think he and Sophie —Sophie's my daughter—work together. They're on my case because I don't go out much. I'm supposed to act like I'm 30 again. But to tell you the truth, I don't really like to leave the house, although I suppose I can sit in here as well as sit in there. And in answer to your question, I'm not sure if there's anything I want from these sessions. I guess I'm supposed to want something, but I'm not sure what it is."

Bart stopped talking and for the first time realized the doctor's desktop was empty. The whole room was empty for that matter. Only bare surfaces and the barren blond lines of Danish modern. No pictures, no photos, no clutter of any sort. Must be his training. He's just told me his life story, but his office shows nothing. A patient photo gallery? No, that wouldn't work. And office stuff or art objects might cause the patient to ask some unwanted questions. My God, Doc, is that a phallus? Bart smiled.

There was a pause. "You retired?" said the doctor.

"Yeah, retired some years ago."

"You did what?"

"I was a lawyer."

The doctor thought for a moment. Bart could sense the doctor's unease. "Tell me about being a lawyer."

"Not much to tell. Can't say I ever loved the law. Bunch of rules. Rules you were supposed to learn and then try to use or get around. Really just learn to figure out how to do what you wanted without getting bitten. If the law's there, it's there. You usually don't know why a law got enacted in the first place.

"It was a game. When you passed 'Go' you got $200. You bought all the railroads and yellow properties if you got the chance. With a little luck, you got hotels and won. And then you put the game away and started another a couple of days or months later."

"And how did that make you feel? said the doctor.

"Feel? Didn't make me feel anything." Bart shrugged, sat back in his chair and looked the doctor in the eyes until the doctor looked away.

"So I'm going to ask you again, what do you expect to get out of these sessions?"

Bart glanced again at the blue clock on the wall. He must not have liked my other answers—or didn't believe them. Five more minutes. He turned to the doctor, "I don't know. Maybe a clue as to why I practiced law in the first place. Maybe I want someone to convince me I did something useful. I suppose I learned something about people. I sometimes doubt it."

"Well, you probably know what I'm going to say. I can't convince you of anything, other than to convince you that you must convince yourself. Anyway, I'm afraid we must stop for today and continue next week."

Bart wondered why the doctor was "afraid". Probably because the "KA-CHING" of his clock had stopped. But he said nothing and went out the secluded back exit of the doctor's office. For some reason he felt nervous, shaky. Too much coffee, he needed something to eat.

Bart negotiated the back steps and slowly walked to his big F-250. He climbed in and started the engine. Without thinking, he put the truck in reverse and backed into the doctor's fence.

Ch 5. Mrs. Higgins

As the night settled in, Bart sat in his office looking out onto the empty field, its green trees turning into black silhouettes. He was hungry but not sure he had anything in the house. He could go out. No, there must be something in the pantry. He flipped on the light. Barren. A can of black olives—the ones with holes that kids put their fingers in. He ordered a sausage and onion pizza. He could dump the olives on top.

He replayed the morning's session, felt like he had undressed in public. With the doctor, he did not feel safe.

Lily soon rescued him with a paw on his knee. She then sat motionless in front of him like a sphinx covered with black fur. He knew she would stare at him until he took her out. Maybe she had to go; maybe not. Even if nature called, she would transition into "What's the hurry? Why don't we walk or play for awhile before I do my business?" So he took her out, played ball in his lighted driveway, then stood guard and cleaned up after her. Back in the house he returned to his comfortable chair; she by his side.

Mrs. Higgins, Bart's neighbor, arrived before the pizza. Dressed in grey slacks and a blue sweater top, Mrs. Higgins held a pie tin in her hands containing half an apple pie. Some of the pie had escaped from its crust. It smelled of cinnamon. Mrs. Higgins, tall, big chested—matronly but a bit sexy thought Bart—offered him the pie. "I had an idea you wouldn't throw this out. Of course if you don't want it... "

"No, I'll take good care of it, and you'll probably get your tin back before morning, maybe even sooner. And thank you," said Bart. "I just ordered a pizza because there was nothing in the house."

"Well you're always welcome if you just want to step next door—that is, if you think you can walk that far."

Mrs. Higgins—everyone called her Mrs. Higgins—had

been a kind neighbor. After Mary died, Mrs. Higgins looked in on Bart from time to time, often bringing him some form of left-over casserole, stew, what have you. Bart welcomed her visits. She was smart, a good cook, cheerful—and someone to talk to.

Mrs. Higgins regularly invited Bart to dinner, though Bart most often found a reason not to go. He enjoyed Mrs. Higgins, but found her husband tiresome. "Higg," who had a masters in mechanical engineering, did not like to talk about music, theatre or current events; he liked to talk about the challenges of heating, ventilation, and air conditioning. And he would talk non-stop if given the opportunity, his slow deep voice delivered at constant pace without inflection. So Bart usually stayed home and Mrs. Higgins, as was the case this evening, came to him.

Bart asked, "Would you like some of this pie? Tart apples. Cinnamon. Flaky crust with large crunchy sugar?"

"No," said Mrs. Higgins. "I swallowed the other half. Have to keep in shape."

"Well I'm sure Higg helped."

Her smile faded. "No. Not tonight. He wasn't feeling too hot."

"Sorry to hear that," said Bart. "Hopefully he'll be better soon."

"Hopefully."

After saying goodbye, Bart began to eat apple pie. Loved the crust and the crunch of its sugar. Would save some for breakfast like they do in New England. The doorbell rang. Pizza delivery. Sausage and onion.

Ch 6. Billy

The following week, on entering the doctor's private office, Bart once again saw the short, muscular man who resembled an outside linebacker for the Rams. Mr. Fitness. He wondered whether shrink was just James' day job.

The doctor motioned Bart to the blond-oak chair. After a few pleasantries, the doctor stopped talking and waited for Bart to speak. Bart refused to play this game, so he watched the clock on the wall until, after a moment or so, the doctor once again asked, "What's on your mind?"

Bart almost said "$200/hour" but did not want to offend the doctor. No sense being nasty. If I don't like $200/hour, all I have to do is leave. He thought the doctor's hourly rate high, but knew his hourly rate as a lawyer had been twice that. He wondered if both he and the doctor were greedy.

Still thinking of greedy, Bart said, "Just now I was thinking of Jack, well not just Jack, Jack and his stepson, Billy. Jack was a client and friend of mine. Somewhat rare with me. I usually didn't make friends with clients. Clients were things that had problems, they were not friends. Usually they were not even people. But Jack was my friend."

The doctor nodded. "Tell me."

Bart sat back, crossed his legs. "Sometime after his first wife died, Jack remarried. Probably, 20 years ago now. His new wife, Susan had a son, Billy, and a deceased daughter, Tanya. Tanya was 16 when she died. Billy was about 10 at the time.

"I mention Tanya because Susan still talked about her when we met for estate planning. For legal reasons, it's necessary during an estate planning meeting to ask about deceased children. Usually clients say something like, 'Yes, we had a son who died at the age of 18, and that's the end of it. But Tanya's memory lived strong in Susan. She adored Tanya, describing her as young, smart, vital. She described her as if she were still living.

"Billy, the living child, was a difficult person and not pleasant to be around—at least according to Jack. Jack said when Billy came around, he always tried to involve his mother in some investment or scheme. At one of Billy's early visits, a visit soon after Jack and Susan were married, Billy told Jack that he really should look at the widow down the street. "She's got money and looks just like Tanya," he said. "You could run away with her and then Mom would forget you as well."

Dr. James looked up toward the window with a slight shake of his head. "Oh my," was all he said.

"Anyway, Susan did her best to keep peace between Billy and Jack. I do think she loved Billy. But at best, Jack tolerated him. Jack said the only time Billy kept quiet was when Billy was sleeping, or someone was talking about Tanya."

Bart stood and stretched. Sat back down. "Sorry, I've got a pulled hamstring that starts to hurt if I sit too long. Souvenir from my trail running days." He continued. "Well, about five years after our initial meeting, Susan was diagnosed with cancer. The disease progressed rapidly. Her doctors could not treat it, only keep her comfortable. At the end she was hospitalized and not expected to live more than a day or so. Jack notified Billy and then asked me if I would be present. He wanted someone there besides Billy.

"On the final day, we gathered, movie-like, around Susan's hospital bed. I remember the antiseptic smell, the white hospital room, and the machines. Cold, it was cold.

"Susan smiled at times, seemed happy we were with her. I can still feel her warm hands and her touch. We all talked to her, and I think she heard us, but she never spoke. And then one of the machines began screeching, an urgent, deafening, screech. The whole hospital rushed in—doctors, nurses, orderlies, all of them came. They tried and tried to revive her. But she was gone.

"A nurse said, 'I'm sorry. She was a lovely person. I'll leave you with her. Please stay as long as you want.'

"We had expected Susan's death. But you know, death is never easy when it comes, expected or not. And for a time in the room all was silent, silent until Billy, with a slight backward glance and raised chin, walked to his mother's bedside, pulled her wedding and engagement rings from her finger, and pushed them in his pocket. Looking directly at Jack, Billy said, "Mom won't be needing these anymore."

"I had to restrain Jack. He said, 'You little shit. Are you that greedy?'"

"Billy just stared at Jack. Looked him in the eye. And then slowly walked to Jack and slapped the rings in Jack's hand. 'Here, old man,' he said. 'I wouldn't want to take anything from you.' He turned and walked toward the door. 'At least you had a turn.'"

Bart stopped talking. Relived the scene in his head. "That's it."

The doctor thought for a time, then, looking at Bart he said, "What did you learn from that?"

Bart pursed his lips. "What did I learn? Not sure what I learned. Billy was hurt and overlooked. He had grown up with a dead saint as a role model. I blame Susan for much of Billy's behavior. That said, Billy was an unpleasant, greedy little prick."

"How did you feel about Jack?"

"I felt sorry for Jack. He was a sad old man who had just lost his wife of 15 years."

"And did you ever feel sorry for Billy?"

"I could understand Billy. He had grown up in the shadow of a ghost. He wanted his mommy and couldn't have her. Did I feel sorry for Billy? No. I couldn't feel sorry for Billy. Billy wasn't my client."

The doctor looked thoughtfully at Bart for several long

seconds. "Finally," he said, "We're out of time."

One week later

Dr. James this morning wears a bright yellow golf shirt, one size too small. Tucked in. He has no stomach, smells of shower, shampoo and soap. His hair is not yet dry. No doubt he brushed his teeth this morning for at least two minutes and thoroughly flossed.

"Good morning," said Dr. James.

Bart nodded.

"Last session we talked about Billy."

"Last session we talked about Jack and the death of his wife. Billy, I think was residue."

"At her death, Billy acted out, took the wedding rings from his mother's finger. According to you, Billy lived in the shadow of Tanya, his deceased sister. Anyway, I asked you about Billy, whether you cared about Billy. And" Dr James referred to his notes, "you said Billy was not your client. So my question to you, did you not care about people who weren't your clients?"

"If they were lively enough, I cared about them. Never turned away from a Miss Young and Vibrant with a welcoming smile and sparkling blue eyes. Of course, that lasted about two minutes until she told me how much I reminded her of her grandfather or great grandfather and then complemented me on my full set of teeth. After one of these conversations I felt like I should be leaning up against a church wall along with the fingernail of St. Horatio and the rest of the relics. And then I would think, 'Enjoy it while it lasts, sweetheart.' I imagined a plum, purple full and plump, turning into a prune, black and wrinkled. No, I didn't. Youth at a client meeting usually brightened my day. I was young once."

"So you cared for Miss Young and Vibrant as you put it.?"

"Sure, but I was not feeling her pain. If she were crying

because her boyfriend had just been killed with a hatchet, caring would rise to another level. And then we would not be talking about caring, we'd be talking about giving.

"Doctor, my principal business was death. Death paid my bills. I organized people's affairs to provide care and avoid taxes at death. When times were lean, I encouraged all of my friends to die so I could handle their estates. Never happened. But I was there for my clients when someone died. I spent many hours sitting with a wife, husband, a daughter while they hurt and cried and questioned and remembered. I spent many hours sitting with children and relatives where they went through the motions of crying, questioning and remembering, until they could tactfully find out how much they were going to get and when.

"I struggled holding myself together for my clients. Never developed the cold dispassion to counsel the world. I had to listen to these people and do the right thing while often their world had collapsed . . . Part of giving is absorbing pain. I often saw myself as a container in danger of overflowing."

Bart shook his head and looked away. Silence took over the room.

After some time, Dr. James asked, "Do you cry?"

Bart at first could not answer. "I don't. . . I can't," said Bart. "I can't cry."

"Why?" said the doctor.

"Once you start. . . . "Bart grasped the arms of his chair, started to get up.

The doctor put his hand out. "We don't have to go there." He sat upright and laid his hands flat on his desk. "So . . . you had no room for Billy?"

Turning toward the doctor, Bart said, "I recognized Billy's situation, his living in the shadow of his dead perfect sister, his wanting the mother's attention he never had. But I couldn't give to Billy. Or rather, I felt I couldn't let Billy take a part of me. There's a difference between recognizing someone's situation and giving a part of yourself." Bart got up from his chair. As he put on his coat, he said, "I long ago realized I was finite—that I only had so much to give. I spent my life giving. I'm done. I'm retired, comfortable in my home. The whole thing may have been useless, but no one can take anything more of me. I'm done giving."

"What about Miss Young and Vibrant?"

Bart smiled, "I'm almost done giving.

Dr. James watched as Bart got into his big truck and maneuvered in the narrow driveway. He wondered whether Bart would return.

Ch 7. Dinner

One Wednesday afternoon, Mrs. Higgins invited Bart to dinner. He as not thrilled. Couldn't imagine spending an entire evening with Higg, not only because Higg was boring, but because he felt Higg suspected him of having feelings for Mrs. Higgins.

Mrs. Higgins sensed Bart's reluctance and assured him all would be comfortable and simple. "Nothing fancy," she said: maybe leftovers or a casserole. She said "Bart you need to get out of the house and into the world. You can clean out your sock drawer some other night."

So Bart agreed and regretted his decision the moment Mrs. Higgins left the house. "Casser-rol-less", wasn't he some famous Spanish chef? But he had agreed and would go. One night. A Thursday. He could do it. Maybe they could watch a baseball game or listen to the grass grow.

Thursday came soon. Bart didn't know what to wear. A sport coat to go next door? Sweats? He finally decided on a plain navy T-shirt, a black fleece, and Levi's. He'd wear actual street shoes to make the whole thing look somewhat dressy and a belt. Of course, he could wear his Rolling Stones T-shirt with the giant red tongue hanging out. No. Don't be an ass.

Bart wore a USC T-shirt under his fleece—a shirt one of Nate's "dates" had given him as a joke. The navy T-shirt was dirty. Bart's Stanford heritage didn't really go with USC's maroon and gold, but whatever, at least it wasn't Cal's blue and gold.

At 6:00 pm Bart presented himself, accepted a bourbon and water, and commenced grazing on displayed hors d'oeuvres sufficient to feed about 10 people. Chips, guacamole, summer sausage, varieties of crackers, cheeses, prosciutto, fruits—a dinner in advance. Maybe he could get a doggy bag.

After several minutes, Mrs. Higgins excused herself and headed to the kitchen. She refused volunteers, said all could help clean up later. Bart was left with Higg who had yet to say more than five words. Higg looked after his retreating wife, then at Bart. Not exactly a deer in the headlights. His gaze was steady. More like the headlights.

Higg sat in a light brown wing chair opposite Bart, leaned back, and commenced what Bart later remembered as a drone, delivered slowly, deliberately and without inflection— a monologue. "Well, I guess you read about the new shopping center we put in downtown Nipomo."

"No, I haven't." Bart tried to sound interested. "Wasn't Nipomo where they photographed that migrant worker and her child—the depression photo on the cover of The Grapes of Wrath?"

"Well, the center is really modern: a long linear shell with interchangeable store space and nothing inside is bearing so you can move walls as you want, which plays hell with the HVAC as you might expect, and you have to redo the calculations every time you change a wall. The first store we put in, Tommy's, sells plumbing supplies, so the heating and air conditioning needs only to be adequate, but it is an interesting business, plumbing business, with the pipe laid out on racks. And then . . ."

"My," said Bart, and thought, this guy doesn't breathe.

"And then the next store sold those little electric carts that people drive around the grocery stores."

"You mean bumper cars," said Bart.

"And you'll never guess what color they painted this store?"

"The color of broken fiberglass?"

"No, beige."

"But isn't everything in California beige?", said Bart.

Higg paused for a second. "And then," continued Higg, "the two stores were a different size, so we had to do different calculations to make. . . "

Bart forced a smile and nodded. He was having trouble keeping awake in the warm room and had a vision of a metronome moving back and forth. . . back and forth. . . back and forth. He shook it off.

"Wow. You must find your job very rewarding."

"Yes, all the different rooms and the calculations, seeing a strip mall come together, not to mention the drawings and dimensions and equipment, it is fascinating, just gets in your blood."

Like HIV or hemophilia, thought Bart.

"I should tell you about the building in Edna where . . . The 'conversation' continued for an additional 15 minutes until Mrs. Higgins threw Bart a lifeline by announcing dinner.

Dinner at last. Mrs. Higgins had outdone herself. Chicken casserole with tortillas and poblano chilis; a red beet salad with arugula, sliced orange and feta cheese; and a chocolate mousse for desert with a touch of Cointreau. All of this Mrs. Higgins served with a chilled New Zealand Sauvignon Blanc. Bart was pleased with Mrs. Higgins' menu and wished he'd laid off the hors d'oeuvres.

Still shell-shocked from Higg's endless monologue, Bart feared the impending conversation, feared that Higg would restart. How could Mrs. Higgins marry this guy? How could she stay married? Had I tortured my guests with the Internal Revenue Code or tax policy? Big difference. My conversations involved more than me. And I can talk at more than 20 words per minute. Also everyone pays taxes. Not sure everyone gets ventilated.

"The secret to success," said Higg, "is concentration of power—focus. I succeeded in business because I focused. When I first looked at mechanical engineering in the county. . ."

Mrs. Higgins cut him off. "Higg, I don't mean interrupt,

but we haven't heard a word from Bart this evening. Could we maybe come back to your story?"

"Yes, of course" said Higg, looking for a moment like he was going to pout.

"Well, actually," said Bart, "I do have a focus story. I'm still famous around the courthouse for my "focus".

"When I first moved to the county, there was only one public defender. So if there were more than one defendant in a criminal case, more than one person accused and being tried, the presiding judge "appointed" public defenders for the remaining defendants from local attorneys—usually from among the attorneys new to the county or most recently admitted to the bar. The judge did not care to hear reasons why an attorney could not serve.

"So, new to the county and a tax lawyer at that, the judge appointed me to defend an assault case where my client, along with several others, had beaten a man with a pool cue. I argued to the judge that appointing me denied the poor defendant his right to counsel under the 6th Amendment, and further, I knew nothing about criminal law. Unmoved, my appointment stood. So, remembering my law school course in criminal law, which I hated, and recalling trial tactics I learned from *To Kill a Mockingbird*, I undertook the defense of my honorable client, a certified low-life with a rap sheet about two inches thick.

"The crime had taken place in a bar. I argued that the victim, let's call him Mr. Smith, was drinking and violent. Smith said he had had nothing to drink. But I had a witness that saw Mr. Smith drinking beer and holding a beer can. And if I could prove him lying, I might sully the prosecution's case.

So, superbly confident, I called my witness. The questioning went something like this:

"Did you see Mr. Smith before the fight?"

"Yes"

"And where was that?"

"It was in the men's room of the bar."

"Could you describe the men's room?"

"Nothing unusual. Three urinals on one wall, a couple of booths on the opposite wall, sinks, paper towels."

"Where was Mr. Smith?"

"He was standing at a urinal."

"And then I asked my killer question that would show Smith had lied and had been drinking,"

"And what was he holding in his hand? The witness just looked at me and said nothing.

"I'm thinking, 'Oh lord, has my witness gone south?'

"So I repeated my question, this time forcefully. I said, what was he holding in his hand?

"The courtroom then went silent. The bailiff snickered and began a controlled bounce in his chair. Muffled laughter in the courtroom. Rolling his eyes, the judge stared at me, slowly shaking his head. "Counsel, maybe. . you. . might. . want to rephrase your question."

"So what happened?" said Mrs. Higgins.

"Well, I'd like to say I immediately rephrased. But it still took me several seconds to understand what I had asked. And finally, I turned red. Asked if Smith held a beer can.

"So, did you win?"

"We reached an agreement with the DA. My client pled to drunk and disorderly, a misdemeanor instead of a felony. Never got to a jury. He got two months in county. But he was looking at two years. So, I guess I won—a reputation if nothing else."

Mrs. Higgins laughed, said, "That's a good story, Bart. At least you made a name for yourself."

Higg did not react, just stared without movement or comment. Said, "Is there seconds on casserole?"

At 8:30 dinner was over. Bart helped clean up and then made his escape. Thanking the combined Higginses, Bart strolled across the small field that separated their houses. Immersed in darkness and quiet, he said hello to Orion who continued his year-long walk in the sky from the east. Bart opened his door, sat in his living room without turning on the lights. Staring out the window at the night sky, he replayed the evening. He really liked Mrs. Higgins, her spirit, her cooking. Liked being with her. But Higg? . . . What a strange combination. How on earth did they ever get together? And why do they stay together?

Ch 8. A Principle to Live By

Despite his misgivings, Bart had enjoyed the give and take with Dr. James, and his initial four sessions had passed quickly. He liked talking about himself if nothing else. Today Dr. James had asked Bart if he had a principle to live by—like "Always be true to yourself" or "Do unto others as you would have them do unto you".

Bart immediately asked the same question of Dr. James, giving examples of "A stitch in time saves nine?" or "Nice guys finish last."

The doctor said, "I try to do more than I promise and give people more than they expect." He said "Giving was life's greatest reward".

"Especially," said Bart, "giving at $200/hour."

"Yes, but you've got to live before you can give."

"Live well to give well?"

"Yeah," said the doctor, "something like that". But we're not talking about me. Let's return to my original question: "Is there an adage or saying that expresses your personal philosophy? —some phrase or sentence or statement you live by? If you had to write Bart's philosophy of life in a sentence, what would you write?"

Bart looked into the distance, exhibiting, as much as he could, a profound search for the words governing and giving meaning to his life.

"I have such a principle. . . but I'm afraid to reveal it. I think you will be angered." Bart paused. "I have enjoyed what these sessions have taught me, but I really think it's best we talk about something else."

The doctor looked skeptical. "I appreciate you're willing to learn more about yourself. Who you are, what you want from this life, are goals of counseling. You should not worry about offending me. We will continue the sessions as long as we both feel I can do you some good. So, say what you will."

Bart hesitated. "OK. This sentence has great meaning for me and expresses my view of life. It's best if you don't take it at face value but think about its inner meaning. Here is my principle.

Bart paused, adopted a solemn demeanor. "Never play leapfrog with a unicorn."

The doctor stared at Bart, trying to decide if Bart were serious. For his part, Bart strained his every fiber to keep from laughing.

"The doctor rested his head on his hands, looked at Bart, then looked down. Finally, put his hands down and looked straight at Bart. "I think you intended to be humorous, but your principle does tell a story. You're talking about self-protection from real and imaginary evils. You're facing both a real evil—the horn. And an imaginary evil--a unicorn. And what is the real evil? I would say a fear of vulnerability. If you play the game —in this case leapfrog--you're likely to get hurt. But you won't get hurt. Unicorns don't exist. And, as is your wont, you have wrapped the entire thing in humor. So, Mr. Jones, assuming I'm correct, what's your real game? What are your afraid of?"

"Aside from you, Doctor, or ill-advised jokes?"

"Both"

Bart did not immediately respond; his humor had left him. After a minute or so, he said, "Exposure. You're taking me out of my armor, showing me to all who would see, including myself. And I'm not sure I want that, not sure what I would see. It's a naked feeling."

"You want to stop?"

"No" Bart paused. "Let's keep going."

Ch 9. The Rock and the Flower

Despite Nate's lack of influence with his father, he checked in with Bart every couple of weeks by phone—usually a "How you doin'?" conversation that Bart immediately shifted to Nate's current love life and business.

In these calls, Nate tried to see where his dad's head was, and find out what was happening in Dad's life, if anything. Today, in response to Nate's question, Bart told him about the therapy sessions. Said the doctor didn't seem to ask much or give any advice. Said it was like paying someone to clean your house but cleaning it yourself. Bart wondered who was doing the counseling.

Bart did say, with a smile Nate couldn't see, that he appreciated Nate's paying for the sessions. Nate, rich and successful, could buy anyone in the family. He lived well, travelled first class. But otherwise, it visibly pained him to spend money and it had become somewhat of a family game to suggest Nate pay for something.

Bart said he certainly wouldn't pay for these sessions, although he really enjoyed talking about himself for an hour. Said he felt like a 3-year-old again. "It's all about me. Really, the doctor should pay me for my stories and brilliant insights."

Nate told him he should wallpaper the house with mirrors so he could enjoy admiring himself 24 hours a day.

"So Dad, tell me about this Mrs. Higgins. Sophie tells me that you've been seeing her."

"Well, you couldn't miss her; she's about six feet tall and probably played rugby scrum in a former life. Sweet woman but you wouldn't want to mess with her. She's my surrogate mother. Brings me apple pies and left-over sausage soup. Checks up on me. Not sure that's 'seeing her' though I did go to dinner at her house last night."

"So the next Mrs. Jones or just a torrid affair?"

"No, she's married and a 'torrid affair' at my age probably means a hot meal and someone to keep the bed warm. No, just neighbors. Don't go over there often. Her husband could bore grass. Think of listening to an audio recording of a math course. Unfortunately, I got stuck with her husband for about 30 hours last night. His voice, I'm not kidding, sounds like a power drill with a low battery. I can't imagine her marrying this guy let alone living with him. There's got to be a story there.

"I did find out she teaches piano and has a degree in music therapy. Not quite sure what that is, whether she counsels poorly written music or uses music to work on your head."

"Could be like aromatics, said Nate. You smell it and feel better."

"Whatever. Anyway, maybe I should take piano lessons. Give me something to do besides watch Jeopardy. And I can find out the secret of the marriage, of the rock and the flower."

"Well, keep me advised. Things happen so quickly with you, what with the couch and the TV, I can't keep up. I'll call you again in a week or so."

"Good plan. Should have news by then. If not, we can talk about doing laundry. Thanks again for the shrink sessions."

Ch 10. Ricky

No traffic on the road today. On the shrink's block, the trees were showing signs of life again. Just pale green buds, but with scent of fresh and new. Sycamores and a few out of place maples. Nice change from live oak. Bart wondered what boy doctor would have up his sleeve this morning; wondered why he still was doing this.

The office was warm and changed somewhat. An exercise bike had been tucked into a corner of the office. "You don't expect me to use that," said Bart.

"Only if you want to." Bart shook his head.

In front of him stood Dr. Anthony James with his impressive physique and tight black T-shirt. Got to be a mirror around here somewhere so he can admire himself. Would James dye his hair when it started to turn grey? Or would he tie it in a ponytail like a 60-year-old trying to be 30? Maybe I should counsel the doctor.

No small talk today. After they were seated, the doctor dispensed with "How are you feeling? And started the session without foreplay. "I want to do something different today. If you can, I'd like you to describe a situation where you have counselled others, where you advised clients whose actions defeated their goals—like, 'I want to lose weight and still eat 5000 calories per day.' It doesn't matter whether you succeeded or not. "The doctor opened his notebook, glanced at the clock on the wall.

"Off to the races, eh Doc? No foreplay today. You're not going to kiss me first? You know, you could save a lot of time if you just told me what you were wanting to discover and asked a straight-forward question—like, 'Do you think your behavior consistent with your goals?' Of course, you don't know my goals, if any, so that probably would be a waste of time, and we'd need to talk about something else for the next 50 minutes. Not that I'm critical of your methods or the time spent. Your hourly rate is cheaper than mine was twenty years ago. In any case, Nate's paying the bill, so I guess I don't care." Bart rested his elbow on the table with chin on closed fist. He said nothing further.

Dr. James fiddled with his pen and his notebook, otherwise did not react. Straight face. No emotion. He looked like the prologue to a fight.

"Bart, you're here—maybe because your kids asked you, maybe because something's not working for you, maybe because you miss your wife, maybe because you've got nothing better to do. I've gone through eight years of training to discover what ails people and what they can do to go forward. It's a bit like the investigation in one of your legal cases, except you look for things and actions. I'm trying to find out what's going on in your head. You need to let me do my job or we're just spinning wheels."

"My head's full of spinning wheels. We seem to be on a road to nowhere." Sensing the doctor's reaction, Bart threw up his hands in surrender. "OK, I apologize. Let's get on with this. I don't know where you're going—losing weight on 5000 calories —or what it's going to tell you about me. When I'm finished, I'd be interested to know what you got, other than your hourly rate. Give me a moment."

Meanwhile, Dr. James said nothing, held the edge of his desk and waited.

Bart knew he had pushed things too far. "So," he said, "clients who act against their interests. Usually clients know what they want: free legal advice that saves them thousands of dollars. But often clients do act against their own goals—usually because the client or the client's husband or wife, really doesn't want what they say they want. A couple does come to mind. Rich doctor and society wife, one of those ladies who lunch. I'll call them 'Doctor Gottrocks and his wife, Doris.' The Gottrocks had money and property—lots of money and property---and they looked the part. The good doctor, portly and outspoken, had a large head and one of those lion manes of grey hair. A big man, his expensive suits yet looked oversized and in need of an iron. He would conduct the entire meeting if you let him. Mrs. Gottrocks rarely spoke. Always wore a dress, usually with a carefully tied silk scarf. I had done a substantial amount of tax and estate planning for the Gottrocks, but at this particular meeting, they came to talk about their son, Ricky.

"Poor Ricky had taken up residency on one of his father's examining tables after losing his current bedroom at San Francisco State. Ricky, it seems, in a moment of gaiety, or drunkenness or both, had thrown a mattress from a fifth story dorm window. Fortunately, he had hurt no one save the pride of the fastidious little campus security guard, Officer Timothy Green, known on campus as 'Green Tim', who wet his pants when the bed landed next to him. Ricky might have made it through his administrative hearing with a suspension, but blew it when he offered to have Officer Green's uniform cleaned and couldn't keep a straight face.

"In the six years since graduation from high school, Ricky married, divorced, and attended four institutions of higher learning, distinguishing himself on all accounts--except fidelity, academics, and judgment.

"At that meeting I remember Gottrocks got right to the point. 'We've always been there for Ricky, given him what he needs, rescued him when he was in trouble. We've gone out of our way to be supportive and understanding. Even replaced the two cars he wrecked. But obviously we've done something wrong. As I told you, he just got kicked out of another school.'

"I remember the doctor solemnly shaking his head and Doris patting his hand. And, of course, he asked me what I would do if Ricky were my son.

"I should have smelled a setup. Normally the good doctor didn't sit back and listen to anyone. And it didn't take a rocket scientist to figure this one out. Someone was looking for support, not advice. Obviously, if Ricky were my son, I would have tossed his sorry butt out and had him working at McDonalds until he came to Jesus. Forgiveness and new cars weren't working. But I didn't say that."

Bart adjusted his chair, stopped talking. The meeting, the setup, still annoyed him. But he had given honest advice.

"Well, what did you say?"

"I gave them a straight answer sanded off at the edges. Obviously, if they wanted to be free of the little darling, then they should show Ricky the door and tell him to find a job. But, as you may have guessed, I didn't make any friends with Doris. She spent the time looking at her lap with her arms crossed in front of her. My stories of enabling, repeating the same action while expecting a different result—went nowhere.

"Finally, when I stopped talking, she looked at me as if I had suggested taking Ricky off life support, which, if you think about it, is exactly what I had done.

"And then Doris came alive, arms uncrossed, face flushed. In a cutting voice she said, 'I don't think either of you understand the situation. And I don't think you can treat Ricky's problems with cruelty. Right now he needs help. That he acts out is not his fault. And we should be supporting him rather than throwing him out a window. You don't stop medical treatment because the cancer doesn't heal as fast as you would like.'

"'Doris,' the doctor pronounced, 'you don't continue the same treatment for the cancer if it's not working. You try something else. The kid will stay a kid as long as we let him. Isn't it time he grows up?'

"Doris was unmoved. Quietly she said, 'I think you're both mean spirited. And I'll continue to help Ricky as long as he needs it.' She got up from her chair, said, 'I'll wait in the car.' And with that the meeting ended. With a disgusted glance in our direction, she put on her suede coat and left. End of story."

Bart looked at the shrink, his shrink, with shaggy hair and perpetual look of concern. James didn't look like a doctor. And neither the blue Danish-modern furniture nor the exercise equipment (nor Bart Jones for that matter) went with a Craftsman house.

"So, what happened?"

"Not sure. They probably got a divorce. And Doris now sleeps on an adjoining examining table where she can reach out to Ricky and touch him. No. I imagine Ricky has enrolled in college #5, Mommy is happy, Daddy is frustrated.

But you know about me; I've died in place. How about telling me how to get off my butt and rejoin the living. As it is, if we just talk all the time, I might stay home and start to smell bad."

"You gave Doris straight advice. How'd that work out for you? Not too well because before the meeting, you didn't know what Doris wanted. If I knew you really wanted to get off your butt, I might tell you how to do that. But if that isn't what you really wanted, I'd be wasting my breath. Like Doris, you'd sit there with your arms crossed. It often takes some exploring before we find out what a patient really wants or does not want and what causes their behavior. What causes the dissatisfaction, concern, whatever, that brings you here and makes you to feel as you do? Once we know, we can deal with it.

"Unfortunately we won't have the answer in this conversation as our time is running out. We should continue talking. I think the outcome will be valuable to you. And I'd ask that you trust my methods—that you let me do what I was trained to do."

Bart wasn't sure about giving the doctor free rein, but the Gottrocks meeting had revealed the feelings of these clients.

Finally, he said, "Well, the Gottrocks probably prove your case. Doris wanted to keep her baby. But until the meeting, I didn't know that, and my advice fell flat. In hindsight, the meeting wasn't about Ricky, it was about the doctor and Doris. In our meetings in this office, maybe we're really not talking about my dying in place but about behavior adult children expect versus what their father might want. My kids have judged my current lifestyle unsatisfactory, disturbing. But like Doris, I may not agree with them, get my coat and walk out. I'm sure you have an opinion."

"Not yet. I don't know what you really want."

Bart left, got in his big truck and went home to his dog Lily. He was not sure how he felt about that session. He missed Mary and would have appreciated her straight advice. When he got home he sat for a time looking around the house. Big house. Big empty house.

After living with someone for almost fifty years, it was tough living alone. Mary had fought a battle she could not win, but kept on. Looked after the house, looked after Bart, looked after the children. Struggled until the very end.

Bart picked up the remote for the TV, thought for a moment, then put it back down. And what have I done since she left? Not much. Not what she would have wanted.

No, Mary would have encouraged counseling, and I'm not sure she would have been wrong. I'm uneasy with these shrink sessions, with James' questions and probing, but I feel alive when I'm there with the give and take, the mental combat. When I'm done with these sessions, I should write a book: "Boy Doctor and the Old Lawyer."

Ch 11. Piano Lessons

Bart played brass instruments in high school and college: tuba, trombone, baritone—finally transitioning solely to trombone and then to nothing when the drunken culture of the college band threatened to end his education. He packed away his lone remaining trombone (he had sold his expensive bass trombone) and carried it from house to house for the next 45 years. A month after his retirement, he took the old silver horn from its orange velour lined case, worked on its slide for a time, and found his embouchure had stayed in college. Selections and pieces from long ago now were now just memories. Too high. Too hard.

For as long as Bart could remember, a piano occupied an interior wall of the house. Nothing fancy, a brown maple spinet Mary played occasionally, and Bart had had tuned from time to time. Later, both children took lessons from a retired local teacher, Georgian by birth, who had studied with Mahler and whose father Stalin had put to death. Like many children, the kids moved on to cross-country, soccer and hormones, and the piano once again became furniture. Over the years, Bart often talked of playing the piano and taking lessons, but did nothing.

On his 68th birthday, Sophie called while he was eating breakfast. All the grandkids were corralled and present on the phone; Nate was conferenced in. The whole group sang Happy Birthday and then presented Bart with six months of piano lessons. "And you'll only have to walk next door," said Nate. "You and Mrs. H can make sweet music together."

"Sure," said Bart. "I'll tinkle her ivories while her husband plays on the black keys." Bart liked talking with the family and feeling the excitement of the grandchildren, but it brought back memories of Mary. Every year she had pretended to forget his birthday only to reveal some extraordinary surprise—a house full of hidden people, a bungee jump (she had opted out), an expensive bottle of Japanese whiskey. "Proscribed Whiskey" she had called it. After she gave him the whiskey, she limited him to an ounce and a half on Saturday night.

"Dad?"

"Sorry. Tuned out there for a second. Wondered if making sweet music would get me shot. "

"Probably just make you tinkle," said Nate. "But getting shot might work too. Might even be a nice way to go, depending on where in the house the murder occurred." Bart said he would rather not find out.

Bart thanked everyone, and after goodbyes and love from the grandchildren, the call ended. He stuck his phone back in his pocket. First the old folks' home, then the shrink, then piano and Mrs. Higgins. What next? A new motorcycle? He liked that idea. But now at 68 and with arthritis in both hands, he wondered about practicing piano and preparing every week. He had never been a flake and wasn't sure he could take lessons "just for fun." But the gift did please him, and he liked the attention--though he wished the kids would give his rejuvenation a rest.

Several weeks later, Mrs. Higgins called Bart to schedule a lesson. At a loss for words, Bart agreed to meet her at her home the following Tuesday at 11:00 in the morning.

Mrs. Higgins' studio, located downstairs from her living room, had its own separate entrance which bore a large sign: "Please take your shoes off before entering." There were floor mats both inside and outside the door, and a chair outside where one could sit and remove shoes. Bart wondered why he needed to remove his shoes to play the piano? The pathway to the entrance was paved and covered, and it didn't snow in San Sebastian.

Whatever. He shrugged his shoulders, removed his shoes and was pleased his socks had no holes. Upon entering the studio, Bart smelled floral disinfectant and noticed a dispenser of "Lavender Clean" on a small table. Mrs. Higgins, wearing fur-lined slippers and a red and white Nordic sweater, welcomed him. She could have modeled for an après-ski poster: "Come relax at China Peak."

"What's with the shoes?"

"Well, you can't play piano with your shoes on."

"Really?"

"No." Mrs. Higgins laughed. "Most of my students are small children. They don't pay much attention to their shoes and what those shoes have gotten into. After replacing the rug once, I opted for socks. Much, much cleaner, but you can take your shoes off inside if you wish. Consider it an adult perk. As to the hand sanitizer, that's also there for the little ones. I try to kill their germs before they kill me, or the other students. I only have a handful of adult students—just enough to keep my sanity. I worked as a musical therapist before we came here."

The studio resembled a cozy den, only lacking a fireplace. A baby grand piano, black and large, dominated one wall of the studio. On the opposite wall a rather extensive music library intimidated all but the most accomplished student. There was a bathroom at one end of the room. At the other end a midi keyboard, recording equipment, and a large, yellowed house plant drooping weakly over a pedestal.

"Nice plant," said Bart.

"It was. . . about a year ago. It can't seem to make up its mind whether to stay or go. I should toss it but feel like I owe it something. Had it a long time."

At this first lesson, Mrs. Higgins discussed Bart's background in music, told Bart how to sit at the piano, and showed him the proper distance from the instrument. She moved his arms to the correct height over the keyboard and, manipulating his hands, gave him a choice of learning to play with flat or curved fingers. She explained that a piano played in both treble and bass clefs, and, given Bart's history of playing low-brass instruments, he would need to learn treble clef. Treble clef was to prove difficult for Bart where the A's were F's and the E's were C's. Unlike most students, he would find the left hand much easier than the right.

At a pause in the lesson, Bart asked, "So how did you come to San Sebastian, small town in our somewhat rural county?"

"Higg took a job with a mechanical engineering firm. The two partners, both in their 70s, later sold him the practice. It worked out well for Higg. Lots of business here and Higg delights in engineering. Would work 24 hours a day if he could. And he's done well. We certainly don't lack for anything, anything material that is." She looked at Bart and forced a smile.

"I grew up in Bertram, Minnesota, a place I'm sure you've never heard of. Hotter than blazes in the summer, and so cold in the winter that you don't set your beer next to a window unless you want it to freeze. Met Higg ice fishing."

And the guy's never thawed, thought Bart but said, "Wow, that's pretty rare."

She laughed. "No, not really, I made it up. I got out of Bertram as soon as I could and never looked back. Bertram born, bred, and fled. Went to Arizona State in Tempe. Chose it because they had a good music program and because it was warm. Also had a scholarship to play softball, which didn't hurt. Met Higg at ASU.

"So, Mr. Jones, what about you? How did you get here? After living as neighbors all these years, I'm surprised we have to ask these questions."

Bart shifted uncomfortably on the piano bench. "Well for a long time, for me, it was all about Mary. We, you and I, were in the background. But to your question, we moved here right after I got out of the state hospital for the criminally insane. Before that, of course, I was the governor of Illinois.

"Right"

"No, nothing so interesting, I was practicing corporate law in New York and bailed in the 70s, looking for a place where I might want to live. That was the return to nature era where people were running around baking bread and eating seeds. I wanted to come back to California and liked the looks of San Sebastian. It didn't have a lawyer on every other block. Mary, my city-bred wife, thought I'd taken her to the end of the earth. Many of the streets weren't paved in those years, and I was young and eager. Lots of changes since then."

They sat in silence for a moment, then with introductions over, they returned to the piano. This time Mrs. Higgins sat on the piano bench alongside Bart, patiently listening to his journey into discord. She corrected his fingering from time to time and encouraged him to play the music without looking at his hands. Bart liked sitting close to her, liked the touch of her hands.

With about 10 minutes left in the lesson, Bart could no longer keep his mind on the piano. Finally, he stopped playing, sat up straight and began to stretch out his back. "Why Mrs. Higgins?", he said. "Surely you have a first name—although I'm told you might be a South American soccer player with only one name--like Fernaldo or Pépé . . . I suppose Mrs. Higgins is better than having people call you Frank or Ralph. Not exactly feminine names. Unique though."

"No, nothing that exotic. My roommates started calling me Mrs. Higgins after I got married, and I just stayed with it. But in a way it beat the alternative. My family, my parents, considered family names a legacy, a link to our ancestors to be cherished and carried on. Some of the family names we can trace back to the 12th century. I'm sure these names were elegant at the time but they, at least in my opinion, have now lost some appeal. For example, I have a brother, Donald, whose real name is Dork. It's one of those names where you say, 'Hi, my name is Dork,' and watch everyone in the room decide whether you're serious."

"So, I take it you got the female version of Dork?"

"Something like that although my name's not that unique and it's not obscene. But to make matters worse, before I married my last name was VanderDonk, which could cause a smirk with any first name."

Mrs. Higgins stopped talking. "Before we continue, I'd like you to play the first two measures of that piece without looking at your hands. You should be able to do it if you keep your fingers on the five keys I showed you."

Bart played two measures—maybe three times. Turning to Mrs. Higgins, he said, "You really don't need to tell me about your name. It's none of my business." But that was not true. He wanted to know all he could about Mrs. Higgins.

"Actually, there's no secret. I don't like one of my names and I don't fit the other. You may have noticed I'm not exactly small. Never been fat, but never small. Although I teach piano, I was always a jock. I lettered in basketball and played starting catcher on my college softball team for three years. Our team went to the NCAA playoffs twice--and I can still outrun most guys I know.

"So, my name. How about Birdie VanderDonk? Elegant, don't you think? Or would you describe it as refined or dainty?"

He smiled. "Maybe you should change your first name to Azalea."

"OK, Mr. Jones. That's enough history for today. Next lesson you answer my questions."

"Works for me, but I do have a serious question. Is Higg OK? I heard something from Mrs. Tharp down the street that didn't sound so good." Bart was sorry he asked the question as soon as he asked it.

Mrs. Higgins closed the keyboard cover and sat still for a

moment. In a quiet voice she said, "Bart, Higg has kidney failure. He has only one kidney and it is diseased. They can't treat it. The doctors say . . . say that he will die within six months without a transplant" Her eyes became vacant, but she made no sound.

"I would think you wouldn't have a problem," said Bart. "It seems like they do those operations almost daily."

"Not when your 70 years old with a history of cancer. The cancer's supposedly gone, but they can't tell us for sure."

"Isn't there some type of national register where you put your name on a list?"

"A kidney register won't touch him because of his age and medical history. We need a direct donor with a specific blood type, and they've ruled me out." Shaking her head in frustration she said, "No, we've got to find someone willing to give a kidney to a 70-year-old who might still have cancer. And we need to find that person within the next six months. I've tried and tried, but so far I've failed."

Bart put his hand on her shoulder. "I'm sure it will work out for you. There must be someone out there who can donate."

"I doubt it, but there's always hope." She sat still, staring at the empty vase on top of the piano. "There should be flowers in that vase." The phone rang. Her next student apparently cancelled. Returning to Bart she said, "I've given up a lot for Higg. I think of what might have been, struggle with my feelings, my guilt. Probably some of the things you felt with Mary. We'll talk someday when this is over. There's probably a donor out there. I just haven't found him."

"Enough about my problems." She picked up the practice book. "#8 for next week," she said, opening the book. "Pay attention to. . . O my gosh, they didn't print the treble—there's no melody." She tapped him with the book. "Guess we'll just have to make up our own song."

After he put his shoes back on, Mrs. Higgins handed him the practice book. "Thanks for your concern for Higg. And yes, you can call me Birdie."

Bart walked across the field to his empty house. He liked the sunshine and the summer smells, liked the sight of the grass beginning to turn golden. As he walked, he thought about Higg, thought about Birdie, thought about himself. He cared about Birdie and did not want to see her hurt. He had strange feelings about Higg and their marriage. But who knows what make people happy?

She had told him Higg would die soon without an organ donation. Bart knew he could donate. Knew with his O negative blood type he could donate to nearly anyone. His donation would help Higg; he wasn't sure about Mrs. Higgins. But then he thought about hospitals and cold and doctors cutting on him. He shivered. . . No. He'd like to help, but really he had no dog in this fight.

Ch 12. Mrs. Tharp/Granny T

To the south of Bart's property, one could see another sprawling ranch-style house which overlooked Bart's home and that of the Higgins. Mr. and Mrs. Tharp built the house years ago and had been its sole occupants. Looking out their front windows, the Tharps could observe the comings and goings of the other properties. Gladys Tharp, named "Granny T" by the Jones children for her age and smothering attention, kept a close record of all that happened on the street, and, as best she could, in the houses. She quickly reported anything she considered suspicious or morally questionable.

Mr. Tharp, "Johnny", soft-spoken and kind, kept the Tharp property clean and trim, and was the "go-to" neighbor for all things in need of fixing. Lawn mowers, dishwashers, you name it, Johnny would help. "You're going to need this part, Mrs. Higgins. I'll pick one up this afternoon and then we'll get this working. And no, I don't need any money. You can pay for the part when I find out how much it is. I'm glad to be of help." An unlikely pair, Bart often said, like a puppy marrying a wasp.

Granny T often started a conversation with something like, "I heard Mary had another bad spell last evening; or "I understand Mr. Smith's problems with the city have gotten worse and he's come to see you." Sometimes what she said was true; mostly she fished for information. Wise to the game, Bart wasn't about to disclose a client confidence or identity to a serial purveyor of gossip. News travels fast in small towns. Aside from the ethics of the situation, breach of trust could seriously harm Bart's legal practice. So Bart would respond, if he responded at all, with "Really?", or "I don't know", or "I was with Mary all night and she seemed fine to me."

As a teenager, Sophie found Granny T beyond nosey. She quickly realized that anything she told Granny T went immediately to her parents and soon could not resist creating wild stories for the ever-inquisitive and confidential Granny to relate. She once told her that Mr. Jensen, the high school 4-H instructor, was caught with a young lamb in the Ag building. That was all she told her. By the time the story reached Bart and Mary, Mr. Jensen and the lamb had exchanged vows. Another time, Sophie cut short a conversation saying, "I'm sorry. I can't talk right now. Condoms go on sale in school today and the ones in colors sell out fast." Shocked, Granny T had a serious conversation with Bart and Mary that evening, who once again had a conversation with Sophie about the dangers of messing with the town gossip.

It was thus inevitable that Mrs. Higgin's trips next door and Bart's visits to Mrs. Higgin's piano studio would come to Granny T's attention. And she wasted no time in communicating her "suspicions" to Higg.

On this morning, Higg sat on his side patio enjoying the sunshine and leafing through Mechanics Illustrated. His feet were up, and a glass of ginger ale sat next to his plastic deck chair. Granny approached, said, "Hi, Higg, I saw you out here and wondered how you were doing? Is everything OK?"

Higg replied that things had not changed, but he was not dead yet and that was good.

Granny said, "You and Bart must be spending a lot of time together. That must be nice for him. It seems like Mrs. Higgins goes over there almost every night."

"Oh, I think she brings him leftovers and such. She felt sorry for him after Mary died."

"Well, I hope it's just that. I began to get worried about you with your condition and all. Just seemed to me that the missus was spending a lot of time next door."

"I'm sure everything's OK. I would know if something were going on."

"Well, I was just worried."

Higg thanked her, then sat for awhile not reading, just

looking at the hillside with its grass turning from green to brown. After a time, he went inside where he found Birdie perched on a kitchen counter, watering a plant she had placed on top of a cupboard. Despite her care, the plant had flattened its leaves against its white pot. "This one may be unhappy," said Birdie. "What's up?"

"Granny T just talked to me. She asked about my condition, wanted to know if you and I were having trouble. She said you go over to Bart's almost every night, and I just wondered if that was true because I go to sleep early although it doesn't seem that often to me but maybe I just haven't paid attention, and of course I have not been myself lately what with being sick and the kidney and all that. I am thinking maybe we should sleep in the same room."

Birdie said, "Whoa. Slow down. Granny says... "

"That you and Bart are together almost every night."

"Birdie's expression, puzzled at first, changed to annoyance. "God, she's such a piece of work. If a problem doesn't exist, she'll create one. No, I haven't been seeing Bart almost every night. I take left-over food to Bart about once a week—sometimes once every two weeks. He comes over here for piano lessons weekly when he doesn't cancel. The lessons last about one hour for which we get paid $195/month. When I take food over there, which I've been doing since Mary got sick, I usually stay and talk for fifteen or twenty minutes. It's 'How you doin'? How are the kids? Brought you some pie or left-over casserole, or whatever, and bye. By the time I get things together, walk across the field and back, check up on you, I probably have spent an hour total."

"Higg, if you haven't noticed, Granny T, sweet thing that she is, feeds on misfortune. She lives for gossip. And when there's nothing there, she creates it. She doesn't need facts, just something to build on, something she can imagine. So Birdie Higgins takes food next door and, throwing her sick husband under the bus, becomes Bart's lover—all in the space of 20 minutes or so every other week with an additional bout every Tuesday on top of the piano. The piano's a challenge because Bart's around 70 or so and doesn't move around so well. Why not? Boy meets girl. And then? Then she tells the sick husband, you, she suspects the worst. And then? And then she tells her suspicions to everyone who will listen."

Higg said nothing. She knew she had she made things worse with this long defense. She should have just blown it off with a short comment about a bored old lady creating gossip. Now she had to clean up the mess she had made. Granny, God bless her, had hit a nerve. Birdie liked Bart, liked him a lot, and both Birdie and Higg knew it.

Still watching his wife, Higg said, "She's next door to Bart, and scans the neighborhood with binoculars, so she must see something."

With a sigh Birdie said, "Get real. Granny T can't see the Jones' kitchen from her house, and I know she can't see ours. She sees you sitting outside, sick and in poor health and vulnerable. And she sees me occasionally walk across the field. That's it. She'd make a good network reporter or national politician."

"Well, I still think we should sleep in the same room."

Raising her voice, Birdie said, "What does sleeping in the same room have to do with Granny T and my bringing food to Bart?"

"Well I just thought maybe we were growing apart and we should try something different."

"She's really got you going, hasn't she? Honey, sharing a bedroom doesn't work with all your medical equipment, not to mention your books and drafting table. You go to bed early. You always have. And I read late and listen to music almost every night. Both our bedrooms are small. We'd be falling over each other and neither of us would get any sleep. Besides, why change things that have worked for us all these years? Plus, if I'm going to have some hot affair with Bart, it won't happen over here. Except for piano lessons, how many times has Bart been in this house during the last three years? Three times? Twice?"

She was still talking too much but couldn't stop herself. Higg looked toward Bart's house as if uncertain with his wife's explanations. Birdie did not visit Bart every night and Bart did cancel piano lessons from time to time. She almost told him she didn't give a hoot about Bart, but she would be lying, and he would know it. What now? Get in Granny's face. That would that only make things worse.

"You know," she said to Higg, "I've been taking food to Bart, well, to Mary and Bart, since Mary got sick. What is that —three, four years? I have taken more food—that is, a greater quantity of food, since your condition became worse because you don't eat much these days. But I can certainly stop."

His look reminded her of a dog, unsure of what her master had done, but loving her nevertheless. "No, you don't need to do that. I think the problem is mine."

Ch 13. Revenge

Wednesday afternoon Bart sat staring at his large desktop computer which currently displayed San Sebastian National Bank's bill-paying website. Bart paid most of his bills automatically in pre-set amounts. But the amounts increased periodically; and periodically, Bart had to change the amounts. Increases, he noted, never were large, just constant and annoying.

That morning the fit Dr. James had asked about "revenge"—the process of getting even. And sitting in front of the computer, Bart couldn't get the session out of his mind. Why revenge? What did revenge have to do with Bart? What did greed have to do with Bart? Every week a story, or analysis of one. He was beginning to feel like Scheherazade, the queen consort in One Thousand and One Arabian Nights, telling the king constant tales to avoid. . . well in her case to avoid death.

At James request, and after some thought, Bart had recounted the story of his client Eunice—a true revenge tale. As to what it taught Bart, or the doctor for that matter, he had no clue.

Bart wished Mary were here to discuss things. She would tell him what she thought, with no frills, no wrapping. And her analysis, more often than not, would be correct. Most likely she would tell him he was overthinking things—he should just go with the flow, let the doctor do his thing. She might tell him the doctor simply wanted to establish trust so Bart could eventually discuss things that really mattered. On the other hand, if Mary were here, he probably wouldn't be sitting in a shrink's office. But she wasn't here, and he wanted to talk to someone about the session. So Bart telephoned Sophie. And realized too late he would need to tell the entire story again.

"Hi, Dad. What's up?"

"Aside from my tryst on the roof with Mrs. Higgins? Not much. This morning my beloved shrink requested a story of revenge. Since you and your brother got me into this, I'd like you to listen to this tale and give me your thoughts."

"Give me ten minutes, and I'll call you right back."

"Works for me." Bart logged out from the bank site, got up and walked to the adjoining TV room with its smell of popcorn and large overstuffed chairs. Sat, waited for Sophie's call; thought about stories; considered again what Mary would say. "Go with the flow she would say. Develop trust."

Sophie called back at 2:00 PM and after some small talk, said, "Well, let's hear this story. When you're done, I'll tell you what I think."

Bart began, "OK, I was asked by the good doctor if I'd ever been involved in revenge, and then to tell him about it."

"Revenge?"

"Yeah, revenge—you know, getting even. So, I told him about Eunice, not her actual name, of course.

"Eunice was an accountant—an accountant and CEO of three auto franchises with an IQ much exceeding her weight. Eunice's knowledge of cars was limited, though she could sell a factory-installed wheelbase as an extra if she put her mind to it. Her husband, Pete, fixed the cars and stayed in the service department. Eunice ran the books, the financing, the employees, the customers and Pete.

"Eunice did not resemble a typical 70-year-old lady. She usually wore a black leather jacket emblazoned with a yellow "Martin Racing" logo, and complemented this ensemble with black Levi's and motorcycle boots. Her face showed scars of youthful acne, and she had that blond straw-like hair that had been bleached one too many times. Eunice would have looked at home tending bar or on the bitch seat of a Harley."

"Sounds like your kind of client. Surprised you didn't hit on her."

"I did enjoy meeting with her. She was fun, not my typical bucks-up client.

"The Eunice-Pete partnership was a first marriage for Eunice; a second marriage for Pete. Marrying at 55, they had no children.

"After retiring from the Air Force, Pete borrowed money and bought a car repair franchise. He loved cars. He could fix just about anything, but he had no head for business and was soon about to lose everything. A friend told him about Eunice, and Pete hired her to run the business finances. After tracking the operations, accounting for inventory and eliminating free services, she made Pete an offer. She would buy half the business on the condition she handle the customers, the collections, the purchasing. Pete would repair cars. Pete accepted and went from living hand to mouth, to solvent, to entrepreneurial, to remarried. The marriage between Eunice and Pete succeeded, mainly because Pete did as he was told.

"Pete had a daughter, Marilyn, an up-and-coming lawyer in Seattle. In Marilyn, Eunice believed, I think, she had found the daughter she never had.

"Some time after Eunice's marriage to Pete, Marilyn separated from her husband. A long, bitter, angry divorce followed the separation. There was no 'let's be friends,' no agreed division of property. The couple battled, complete with bruises, restraining orders, and massive expense on both sides. At the end of the affair, both players, broke, damaged, and bitter, went their own way. There was no justice, only resolution.

"During the divorce Marilyn called Eunice and her dad almost daily, speaking with whoever answered the phone. After the divorce ended, Pete and Eunice helped Marilyn get back on her feet. They gave her money to get reestablished. Bought a house with her in Seattle. Pete and Eunice owned one half; Marilyn owned one half."

Bart stopped speaking. "You still awake," said Bart.

"Awake and awaiting chapter 2."

Bart continued, "Well when Pete died, Eunice called Marilyn to discuss funeral arrangements. There was some disagreement from the beginning because Marilyn wanted the funeral in Seattle, though Pete had never lived there. She said she was involved in a serious legal case and couldn't afford the time to come to California. Eunice understood the difficulty, would work around Marilyn's schedule, but explained that everyone who knew Pete was in California. So, despite Marilyn's objections, Eunice made arrangements locally. She offered to hold a separate service in Seattle, but Marilyn refused. "

"So Marilyn didn't come to her father's funeral?"

"No, she did. I'm getting to that. There was a funeral, your standard funeral with church service, celebration of life, graveside, flowers, crying, speeches about Pete, his life and idiosyncrasies. Marilyn came, participated and stayed in California an extra day to discuss things with Eunice.

"The discussion took place in Eunice's small office. According to Eunice, Marilyn said she wanted to take care of some business items before returning to Seattle. And her first question was, 'I'd like to know what you intend to do with the business?'

"Eunice said at first she was surprised by the question. They had just buried Pete the day before. Eunice remembered saying, 'I'm not sure I know what you mean.' And Marilyn answering, 'Well, do you plan to sell it, or are you going to buy me out?'

"The loving stepdaughter," said Sophie.

"Yes, the loving stepdaughter. Eunice told Marilyn that she and Pete were joint owners of the business and he had left his ½ share to her. Eunice said she intended to run the business as usual until no longer able and would transfer or sell the shops at that time. She said Carlos, Pete's long-time assistant, would continue running the service portion.

"Eunice said Marilyn, in a visible struggle for control, accused Eunice of stealing. In an icy pointed manner, she said her father paid for these shops from his Air Force retirement and from the monies he and her mother had saved. Eunice said she tried talking to Marilyn, hoped she would settle down. She told Marilyn that when she joined the business there was only one franchise and it was on the verge of closing. Pete had mortgaged his house and spent almost all his savings. The shop was broke. Pete couldn't pay his bank loan. He couldn't pay himself. He was close to losing both the shop and his house. She told Marilyn she had invested her savings in a failing operation, put Pete in the shop servicing vehicles, and ran the operation as a business. It succeeded. They used the profits to buy two more franchises."

"Eunice described Marilyn as flushed and shaking. Said she thought for a moment Marilyn was going to attack her. 'She got right in my face: 'You're not going to get away with this,' she said. 'I talked to my father every week. I know what was going on and I know what he told me. My dad didn't lie. I want what's mine and you will not cheat me. I have unlimited legal resources and will do what's necessary to get my share.'

"Marilyn then returned to Seattle. Several weeks later Eunice received a letter from a lawyer threatening to sue unless Eunice '. . . made arrangements to pay Marilyn for her share of the business.'"

"So what did you do?"

"Well I knew that Marilyn could not win such a suit, nor could she support it financially. Pete and Eunice held the property in joint tenancy with right of survivorship, had been married for 15 years. When Eunice invested in the business both she and Pete had their own lawyers, and further, Eunice's financial contributions were documented. So basically, after an explanatory letter, I did nothing. Nevertheless, for months Marilyn and her lawyer continued to threaten.

Marilyn called Eunice a gold-digger, dishonest and immoral for depriving her of her inheritance. Marilyn said, 'Of course financial transactions were documented. Guess who was the accountant?'

"Hold on," Dad. "I've got a kid situation here."

"Sure," said Bart. He realized his story had taken a long time and wished now he had not called. When Sophie returned, he told her he would try to cut it short, but she wanted to hear the whole thing. So Bart went on.

"Before the funeral, Eunice and I had talked about what she wanted to do with her estate—the auto franchises, her homes, investments and belongings. Eunice had a sister, but the sister had an estate of her own and was older than Eunice. So Eunice thought she would leave things to Pete's daughter, Marilyn, maybe with one of the shops to Carlos, Pete's right-hand man for many years. Obviously, things had now changed.

"After these threats started, I spent some time with Eunice. I remember one conference in particular, remember it because Eunice, a tough strong lady, had tears in her eyes. She said, 'We were married for 15 years. I thought I had acquired a daughter, but I guess I didn't count for much. We constantly helped her, both financially and with her divorce. I spent hours listening to her rants about her husband, his nastiness and how badly he treated her. I sent her little things to cheer her up— a card, a scarf, an email, just some things to let her know I was thinking about her. I now believe her husband may have been the victim."

"Hold on," said Sophie. "I'll be right back—Tom's going to pick up dinner. Want to make sure it's not 100% comfort food." She came back out of breath. "Sorry, go ahead."

"Yeah, it was not fun. It was one of those conversations where you can't do anything but listen. But Eunice sucked it up, 'Oh, well,' I remember her saying, 'I'm a big girl and it's only money. I was going to leave most of my estate to her."

"And then I almost laughed out loud." I said, "You know," there's one thing you could do, call it an acknowledgment of Marilyn's 'kindness' to you when Pete died."

"What," said Eunice. "Tell me".

"I said, 'Well, you own one half of Marilyn's house. What if you were to deed that one half to Marilyn's ex-husband?'"

"Oh, Dad, you are wicked."

"Eunice and I both started laughing. It was a delicious idea, don't you think? Pure revenge. And nothing Marilyn could do about it. Perhaps justice for once instead of resolution."

"Dad, you are evil."

"I loved the idea."

"So what happened?"

"Well, after a good laugh, I gave Eunice time to think about it and in the meantime had a deed prepared to Marilyn's ex. Several weeks later we met again. Eunice said she loved the wickedness of the idea and loved thinking about it. Said it was tempting. But in the end she wouldn't do it.

"She said, 'Marilyn has lost whatever family she had. I think we should deed the one half to Marilyn and be done with her. I love the thought of revenge, but I will sleep better with forgiveness. And who knows? She might send me a thank-you note.'"

"That's a quite a story," said Sophie.

"Yeah, it's certainly different. But what was the shrink's purpose in having me tell it? What does this story tell the shrink about me? What did I learn?" Bart had enjoyed telling the story, but it made him feel uncomfortable, probably because he had never brought up forgiveness.

"I don't know. Maybe you need to wait until the next appointment. You haven't gone to that many sessions. He may still just be trying to establish trust. Reach a level where you're comfortable confiding in him."

"But why revenge?"

"Why not? Or, as I said, wait until next week and ask him."

An hour later Bart received an email from Sophie:

To Bart; cc to Nate.

Dad, I couldn't help thinking about our conversation, the revenge story, what it means. I'm concerned you had to call me to have someone to discuss it with. I don't want to hurt your feelings. You're my dad and I love you. But you really need someone to talk to besides Nate and me. You're alone in that big house, and your social life, as far as Nate and I can tell, consists of a married neighbor and a shrink. Despite our 10-year agreement, I think you really might consider looking into a retirement community where you have someone other than Nate and me to talk to. You're 68, you're still in good health. Nate and I have discussed this, and both think this might be a good idea or at least something to consider. We both worry about you. It's especially worrisome 3000 miles away and with Nate almost never home."

Bart responded,

Well I've always liked those nursing homes. And they always have deals on used carpet.

Sophie replied:

No, a high-end retirement campus liked the Sycamores. Places where intelligent interesting people live. People like Stan, the guy you met there. A resort, not a warehouse. A place that offers independent living as well as assisted living and medical care as people need it. You could own a residence there and travel or isolate yourself as much as you would like. But you'd have people around, activities, social life if you wanted it, and maybe a few potted plants as well.

This time Bart sent a text in reply.

Sophie, these places give me the creeps, the Sycamores gave me the creeps. A bunch of old people playing bingo and taking two hours to eat half a sandwich. You're talking about God's waiting room. I know you're concerned, but the scene terrifies me. Give it ten years and we'll talk again. Sorry I bothered you.   One Week Later

Heavy fog this morning. Trees outlined, no branches, green blending with black. Bart sat in his office, cold, thinking about everything and nothing. Last week he had discussed revenge with Dr. James and had told the story of Eunice. Eunice, upbeat and cheerful. Eunice with her black motorcycle boots, pock-marked face, and leather racing jacket. Unique but beautiful in her own way.

Bart walked outside. He had lived with fog his entire life, but in the damp and obscurity of fog, the smells of earth, grass, and oak remain as if saying, "We're still here. You may hide us in your wet and grey, but we're still here."

Later that day, Bart met with the boy-doctor and asked about revenge, the topic of the prior week. Actually, he asked about revenge, lust, envy and the other deadly sins. Would the doctor cover all seven? Did he have a checklist? Bart remembered thinking, OK revenge. Why not lust? Or something dear to his heart like sloth?

With utmost seriousness, the doctor said he was saving lust 'til last, figuring it would get them through sloth. It would be a reward after covering the prior six deadly sins—the light at the end of the tunnel. The doctor said revenge, not the most milk-toast of emotions, leads to discovery. For starters, he said revenge is a strongly felt emotion, not an emotion out in the sun on a lazy summer day. It's humiliation, a slash to the face. The desire to get even, said the doctor, can reveal people and events that need to come out.

But he said Bart outwardly appeared not shackled or clouded by revenge. When asked about revenge, Bart did not talk or think about his own feelings, but of a story where he suggested revenge to someone else, where the game ended with forgiveness. The doctor's question merely caused Bart to recall an amusing story with a client. But the doctor couldn't be certain. He said that Bart often guarded his feelings. Defended the end line with a ball bounced back in another direction.

Bart thought about this. He had been honest about his feelings. In the story of Eunice, revenge would have been justice.

For once, justice. As a lawyer, most often justice played second fiddle to resolution. He often told clients, "You can be right, or you can end this and go forward with your life. I think you'll prevail, but being right will cost you a lot of anger and a lot of money. Hard to accept, but a settlement's really in your interest." Eunice had a rare opportunity for justice, a chance to be right swiftly and without expense. Instead, she chose forgiveness and resolution.

Did Bart want revenge? Did he blame Mary for his sitting alone at 68 years in an empty house? No. The children? He didn't like the involvement of Nate and Sophie—especially their view that he should take up a wheelchair in an old-folks home or alternatively run the 400-meter hurdles at the next Olympics. But he'd practiced law long enough to know that any child's view of their parents was completely insane.

No. No revenge.

Bart Jones knew he always had reaped what he sowed. Maybe he preferred his fields to go fallow. Maybe. He raised up from his office chair. The fog had lifted. Through his office window he could see the dry field behind his house, and the little oak waving its new leaves in the wind. He smiled. A silent cheer.

Ch 14. Birdie

Piano lessons were hit or miss with Bart. Despite his abundance of free time, some weeks he simply did not practice. Mrs. Higgins, perpetually tolerant and used to dealing with children, always found something positive to say: "You really played that measure well," or, "You have an excellent sense of timing." In his case, Bart thought a better comment might be, "Of all the piano students I have ever had, you are one of them."

On this August morning, the fog had cleared, opening the day to warmth and sunlight. Walking across the damp field, the ground still stuck to his shoes, but he could now see the trees at the back of the field. When he arrived at Casa Higgins, he took off his shoes as usual, entered the studio and sat next to Mrs. Higgins on the piano bench. He had no interest in playing the piano, wondered if they could just talk.

This had happened before, but only brief and occasional stories between practice pieces: odd clients, funny students, college sports, his time in the Marine Corps. This morning, without looking at her, he asked how she and Higg had gotten together. "You seem like an unlikely pair."

She responded with a slight shake of her head. "No," she said, "you're not getting off that easy. You must play before we can talk. You don't have to play long, but you must play. Your kids didn't pay me to teach you the history of Birdie VanderDonk. If you play well, I might answer your question."

And so he played: he struggled for about twenty minutes, his music sounding somewhat like a seagull with its feet caught in a garbage disposal. "I'm sorry," he said. "I'm not with it this morning. Feel a bit like your ever-dying plant over there."

"Yeah, I probably should get rid of it, but, as you know, I've had it a long time."

"You do have to admire it for hanging in there. Maybe you could sell it—you know, sell the last two weeks of a great plant."

She put her hands in her lap, looked up at Bart. "I take it we're finished playing,"

"Yeah, I think we're back to life story."

"Well, I'm going to get off the bench if we're not going to play. I'll tell you about Birdie VanderDonk." Birdie moved to a chair and sat for several seconds as if trying to gather her thoughts. She stared at Bart, perhaps reconsidering whether to share her private world.

Bart felt her struggle, feared they--Bart and Birdie--had gone too far. He had asked her to open a door that once unlatched, could not be closed. "We can stay with the music," said Bart.

"No, I want you to know this." Birdie clasped her hands and held her arms tightly to her sides as if she were cold. "Arizona State was my first real trip away from home. From the steamy summers and frozen winters of Bertram, Minnesota, to the dry red and brown Southwest with its sandstone and cactus. I had a scholarship to play softball, a full ride, provided I maintained a B average and was of good moral character—meaning at that time in America, I didn't steal, smoke pot, or get pregnant. Softball was my escape. I could throw out a runner at second base and guard home plate better than anyone. I could also hit.

"ASU opened another world for me. Not just sunshine and cactus, but people, people my age. Eager 17 and 18-year-olds, all seeking something new, getting out of Dodge.

"I met Ralph Barker the first week in Tempe. 6'3", a showy Texan with a white shirt and big silver buckle. Friends called him "Bite". He had an easy manner like someone rich and powerful. There were flowers, fast drives though the desert in his yellow Jaguar XKE, concerts. I think you can guess the rest. Toward the middle of my second semester, I got pregnant, and my big Texas boyfriend went home to Daddy.

"Unmarried girls didn't get pregnant in those days. They

either disappeared or hid and got talked about. If they had money, they would have the baby discreetly and put it with someone else to raise, usually parents. If not, the girl would have the child and live under a cloud, as would her parents' family. Terminating a pregnancy, abortion, was not legal. Besides I was Catholic."

"What about the father, said Bart? What about Bite?"

"Nothing. Gone. In those days, things were not fair. Maybe they still aren't. As my mother would say, "Life isn't fair. Fair is where to take your pig.

"Anyway, I knew once my condition showed, I would lose my scholarship and find myself back in Bertram, a single mother facing a difficult future. With luck I'd marry—a local boy also without a future."

"Oh my God, Birdie, what did you do? I can't imagine. . . "

"I didn't know what to do. I first thought of taking a leave of absence from ASU—a 'family situation calls me home'—have my parents raise the child and come back to school the following year. But I couldn't do it. It would have been unfair to them and caused a ton of small-town talk and embarrassment.

"Then Martha, my college roommate called Higg. I had met Higg in the registration line during the first day of school. He stared at me so much I began to get embarrassed. Nice, polite person, but different, strange. Today we would say he was on the spectrum. Academic genius but a social moron. I ran into him frequently during my first year and found it difficult to shed him. He was a big puppy dog wanting to be with me. Martha heard more Higg stories from me than she ever wanted.

"Anyway, Martha explained my situation to Higg. Higg found me the next day and offered to marry me. Just like that. Came over and said we should get married. He said it would be a 'marriage of convenience', but we would raise the child together. So we did. Drove to Las Vegas—no waiting period, no blood test

—and married. And about a month later, after a softball game, I miscarried. Continued playing softball during the season as if nothing had happened. Higg studied his engineering, getting A's in statics and dynamics; coming around frequently to see how I was doing. I thought we would get the marriage annulled, but we never did.

She looked at Bart, "Guess you think I was stupid?"

He looked at her wide-eyed and slowly shook his head. "No, between a rock and a hard place."

"Whatever, for the next three years, Higg was never far away. I helped him as much as he helped me. He looked after me; I socialized him. We grew closer as time went on. You might say I had an arranged marriage—self-arranged by a scared 18-year-old.

"Higg's been a faithful roommate. He's always been there for me after my one great adventure into love. He's devoted, provides well, doesn't leave his clothes lying around. Anyway, we have stayed together. Now he's about to go away."

Bart, showing a look of concern and knowing he could help, said nothing. He crossed his arms in front of chest, then catching himself, put his hands on his legs.

Birdie looked out on the dry field. A couple of ravens croaked in the distance. She looked back at the black and white keys of the piano. "Things are black and white until you mix them. Then you get a beautiful song or the sound of a raven. And by the time you know what will work and what won't, you don't play anymore.

"I married because I was weak and scared. I stayed married because I was weak. I'm afraid to play now, as much as I'd like to."

Neither knew how long Higg had stood in the doorway to the studio. Had he heard Birdie's confession: that she stayed married because she was weak.? Had he seen his wife, his treasure, talking quietly with Bart in the small studio? Higg said, "I came to tell you you're 12:00 cancelled." He bowed his head and left. Somewhere in the distance, a phone rang. Birdie spoke first. "I'd better go."

Ch 15. Gladys Tharp

Instead of the park trail, today Bart walked on the street so they—Bart and Lily—didn't track mud into the house. With luck, the fog would be gone by 10:00 and all would be sunny and warm. Bart liked the fog when he wanted to sleep in. The rest of the time it acted like a guest who didn't know when to leave.

At 18 months, Lily bound along seeking the perfect place to do her business. At 68, Bart sleepwalked, wishing she had a bigger bladder or he had fenced his yard. Maybe. . . maybe they make Depens for dogs. Maybe there's a service that will take the thing off after she has done her business. Of course if he stopped feeding her . . .

Bart could see the park trail from the street, decided to take it anyway and worry about mud later. Sometimes he just didn't like civilization, and walking on streets surrounded him with it. He always looked forward to the park and the freshly washed smell of the trees and grass, and he knew at this hour he would be alone. It was not to be.

"Bart, good morning." A smothering voice. Saccharin. God, thought Bart, what luck. On one side Higg, with his infinite loop tape of inane conversation; on the other side the unctuous grand inquisitor.

"How are you, Bart? And how is Mrs. Higgins?" She stretched out the second question with an uplifted voice.

He kept a straight face. A slip or misstep would turn Bart and Mrs. Higgins into a passionate affair. Still he had to resist telling her they'd done it last night between the houses, and how he'd spent the next hour picking fox tails out of her butt. No. No end of trouble. She'd believe it. "I'm a little cold this morning, Gladys. Should have taken my walk after the fog lifted. But Lily had other. . . needs, and of course she wears a fur coat. This parka's seen better days. How are you doing?"

"I'm fine" said Gladys, "I wanted to ask you about. . . "

"Bit of a rush this morning," said Bart. "As I said, I've got a dog with a need." He smiled, gave a short wave and started to walk.

Not to be put off, she said, "I thought you could tell me about Mrs. Higgins. You see her quite a bit, don't you?"

He stopped and turned around. "I see her once a week for piano lessons—that is, when one of us doesn't cancel. Last Tuesday she was fine. She's got her hands full with Higg." Once again he started to walk.

"And how is Miss Lily?" Lily, Bart's standard poodle, sat patiently by his side.

Bart stopped, looked Gladys in the eye. "She suffers from flatulence, Gladys, and the older she gets, the more gas she has. I can really see the connection between old and fart, and I think it's because she gulps her food, although I am training her to eat more slowly—you know, to sip rather than gulp, but so far she hasn't responded. I say, "Go sip, go sip" and she just tilts her head and looks at me like I'm an idiot." He reached down and noodled Lily's head. It was too early in the morning for Gladys. There were other rocks she could look under.

Granny had lost her cheeriness. "Well, maybe you should get a cat."

"I had a cat. Big blond Persian with a flat face and yellow eyes. Dumb as grass. The thing continually puked up hairballs, usually on an upholstered chair. Can't tell you how many wet cheeks I got sitting on hairballs. You ever sit on a hairball, Gladys? They're always soaking. Take a long time to dry out."

Gladys' eyes flattened. Bart looked at her and smiled. Raised his eyebrows and awaited a response.

"I must be going," she said. I'm going to the café for breakfast with my friend, Joan. I'll tell her what you said about Mrs. Higgins."

"And what was that?" said Bart.

Gladys didn't respond but hurried away and nearly fell over a trash can.

"Anyway, if you've got any ideas for Lily, please let me know."

Gladys continued walking and said nothing. Lily looked up at Bart and tilted her head as if to say, "What was that about?"

"Bartholomew Jones and Mrs. Higgins," said Bart. "Probably the X-rated version. We'll need to wait a week or so until Gladys passes her exposé around the circle. I'm sure it will be juicy. I shouldn't have lost it with her. She can spread rumor faster than a network news reporter."

Ch 16. Invisible

Bart sat surrounded by his large "oak" desk, doing nothing in particular. Through his office window he could see the empty field at the back of his house with its dead grass and twisted trees. His desk really wasn't oak, but Formica that looked like oak, or some such wood. The huge L-shaped thing occupied two entire walls of his small white office and was littered with yellow pads, old law books, and various office junk: clips, pens, staplers, an old Rolodex. On the walls of the room hung framed postcards of France and Germany--Honfleur with its sail boats, and Rothenberg with its orange roofs. A framed poster advertised the 1996 opening performance of the local arts center.

Outside there was no wind, just dust, parched grass and heat. A small oak grew outside Bart's window. About 1' high, its light green leaves verdant against the brown grass. New oaks grew every spring, but rarely lived more than a season or two, victims of the heat and dryness of the summer. Nevertheless, despite the odds, one or two sprouted each year, waving their green flags, hoping to grow and thrive. Bart admired their courage.

Mary had been gone for two years. She had worried about Bart. Said he didn't seek out other people and had few friends. Bart just shook his head. He was content to be alone. But Mary claimed that big strong Bart, a mighty oak with his quick wit and humor, hid another person: One who cried in movies, who couldn't read sad stories aloud. One who "loaned" money when people needed it and took in trash for the old people next to his office. But Mary worried. "What are you going to do when I'm gone? You've only got one friend—me."

Bart often saw people as an imposition, a burden, things that occupied his time without purpose. He usually just let Mary talk. Her friendships and social activities were important to her and that was OK, but he didn't share her feelings.

Things changed once Mary left. The travel, the performances, the dinners out ended. He now found travel and concerts— "activities"—tiring. Well, not the events themselves —the getting ready and the going and the coming home with no one to talk to. Often, Bart, lacked the mental energy to "get ready" and would give away tickets, or just not use them.

Bart couldn't remember why he had sat down at his desk today. Just something to do he supposed. He looked out on the small oak, wondered if it would succeed.

Mary, with her royal "we", always had prodded him to act. "We need to call Mrs. Brown about that antique desk", or "We need to move that old weight set out of the garage, so I don't constantly run into it." In other words, "Call Mrs. Brown about the desk; get the weight set out of the garage."

Bart realized he had changed. His video had become a painting—one of those faces frozen in the National Portrait Gallery. Identified but unknown. "Colonel Benjamin Marks, 1822. Marisa Dunwoody, 1831." Faces you stand in front of and try to figure out what kind of person they were. Kind, mean— beloved, lonely? Arrogant? Humble? Did they love? Were they loved? No one remembers.

No portraits here in the 21st century. You just become invisible and soon no one remembers you. So maybe the time to live is now, to move, get in shape, reconnect with the world. Like the little oak, I might not survive another dry season.

Ch 17. Decisions

Later that day, Bart walked across the field carrying his piano music in a small black canvas briefcase that some insurance company had given him. He should have walked down the street, less dust, but the trail was shorter. The grasses were tall this year for a change as a result of the rainy winter. Bone dry now in the hot summer; they were full of foxtails. He would have to check Lily's paws after each walk.

Bart climbed down the short slope to the Higgins' concrete walkway, sat in the white patio chair, and removed his shoes. Someday he'd have a public performance and wear socks with gigantic holes in them, or maybe white socks with black pants. He opened the slider. Mrs. Higgins sat at the bench playing something difficult—Chopin probably. She looked up at Bart and smiled through wet eyes.

"Problems?" said Bart.

"Yeah, same problem." She closed the piano and rested her hands on her lap. Turning to Bart, she said, "He's dying, Bart, and all I can do is watch. I can't donate, and I've found no donor. But I can't blame people. Higg's an older man with a history of cancer. People want to give a future, not just a chance. So life goes on—or doesn't, I suppose. Anyway, you don't need to hear any of this."

Bart said he was sure things would work out. He felt her doubt, her bleak outlook, but was convinced he could help. He wanted to help. This was just a problem to be solved, and he could solve problems. Clients had paid him to solve problems.

For the rest of the hour, Bart acted as if all were normal, and offered various excuses for his lack of practice. ("I had to clean the lint screen in the dryer; Lily ate my music, &c.") Mrs. Higgins ignored him, encouraged his playing. She told Bart he had improved and to keep at it.

After the lesson, Bart re-traced the trail across the

browning field. He had had a piano lesson, but now saw only Birdie and her tears, saw Higg with his need for help.

The little green oak broke his reverie. One foot of greenery against the odds. Water it and tilt the scale? Good or bad? Bart didn't know. But he cared about it and wanted it to survive. Would he lessen, diminish the oak's victory if he watered it? Probably. He would think about it.

Once a year Bart, like many men his age, met with a urologist, a member of the "stream team". Urologists treated such things as the frequent need to pee—a condition causing sleepless nights, many travel stops, and social interruptions; enlarged prostates which could reveal cancer; inadequate flow which made that 2:00 am visit seem like sunrise would occur before completion; and, of course ED— "Call your doctor if you have an erection lasting more than four hours". Every man's dream thought Bart.

This afternoon, still thinking of Birdie, Bart had his annual checkup, a less-than-pleasant experience where he would "produce" a sample, answer questions about flow, incontinence and ED; and bend over with pants down while the doctor probed his lateral region and felt his prostate.

Bart's urologist, along with about five others, maintained a second-floor office in a medical building adjoining the local hospital, "Sierra Peak Health." The Urology Group had a large waiting room filled with rows of back-to-back chairs in which sat mostly men, many of whom had passed their sell-by date. A glass enclosure at one end of the room guarded the receptionist. It reminded Bart of looking at a fish through water.

Every year the receptionist, "Marge", handed Bart a clip board, pen and 10 or so sheets of a double-sided questionnaire.

There were multiple check boxes opposite various diseases most with Latin and Greek names. Bart could choose "yes", "no", or "N/A." "I haven't a clue" wasn't a choice. So, Bart dutifully checked "no" to everything while fighting the temptation to answer "yes" to all these diseases and conditions, just to see if anyone read the thing.

After filling out this wonderous package, Bart returned to the receptionist where he was asked for his Medicare card, his driver's license, and proof of any additional insurance he might have. Marge then made copies, and, after having taken several phone calls, returned the originals to Bart and asked him to take a seat. Elapsed time from entry into the waiting room: about 40 minutes.

Twenty minutes later, a large nurse, who had learned English only the prior year, loudly called "Bartholomew" or a facsimile thereof, causing all eyes in the room to pretend not to look. Bart then arose and was escorted to a bathroom. There he was told to pee in a plastic cup with a lid (the lid went on after the pee) and put the filled cup in a faux medicine cabinet that had a back door which opened to the nurses' station.

After "producing this sample", a nurse conducted Bart to a private waiting room, told him to take a chair, and said the doctor would be right with him. In other words, "wait". Of course wait, doctors are busy, and their time is valuable.

About 15 minutes later, Dr. Richard Peterman, "Dr. P" according to Bart, rushed into the patient room in a starched white flourish and asked Bart how he had been, a question, no doubt, the good doctor had been taught to ask in med school. Ignoring the answer, he immediately began typing on his computer. Bart replied, "I'm thinking of donating a kidney."

"Do-nat-ing a kidney. That's nice. Dr. P continued to type. — "What? You're kidding?" Dr. P turned from his computer and suddenly regained consciousness. He considered Bart and, after a short time, said, "Well. . . there is no prohibition against donations by people your age. . . provided you're in good health: No diabetes, no cancer, no HIV, hemophilia, or mental illness. You will need to lay off the sauce and keep up your exercise." Returning to his computer he said, "And you have O negative blood, which means you're a universal donor. As far as I can see, you're in good health and can give a kidney to anyone. You should talk to your regular doctor though. I'm sure he or she will tell you the same thing, but they will know more about your physical condition." Dr. P shook Bart's hand. "Giving a kidney saves a life. It's a noble thing to do."

After stumbling on a chair, Bart made his way to the reception area. He had expected his age would disqualify him from donating. He hated hospitals and shuddered at the thought of some doctor cutting him open. For a while he sat in the corner of the waiting room thinking of Birdie and Higg, of knives and nobility, of cowardice and dishonor. Looking around, he felt like the entire waiting room watched him. Was this a test? He hadn't committed, hadn't talked to Birdie. She would never know.

He made his way to reception, scheduled his next annual appointment, and went home.

Ch 18. Life with Mary

For the next therapy session, Dr. James had said he wanted to talk about Mary. Thinking what—that Mary's dead hand controlled Bart from the grave? Bart missed Mary, thought of her often, but wasn't sure what he could add to that. As he pulled onto the doctor's street, Bart saw his friendly jogger ambling toward him in his running hat and Clovis half marathon shirt. This time he waved, then drove around back, carefully avoiding the fence. Once upon a time he feared these meetings, feared someone would see him, believe him weak. He looked forward to them now, a chance to talk about himself for a whole hour. Sort of like sex for money, but 45 minutes longer and he wouldn't be naked, well at least not that kind of naked.

The good doctor was there as usual, scrubbed, wet and smelling of soap. What's his thing Bart wondered? An example of discipline and good health, or an exhibitionist? Maybe he was gay. Whatever. He didn't care.

And so Bart told Mary's story to Dr. James. It took up much of the session and Bart knew another Mary session, an analysis, would follow.

Mary had died of cancer, first diagnosed about two years before her death. When they got the news, she assumed the worst and immediately began planning. Bart must learn to cook so he doesn't just eat PB and J or cold stuff straight from cans. She subscribed to Healthy Fresh, a meal delivery service with ingredients and step by step instructions on cooking. Bart got the "opportunity" to cook dinners, with Mary's skilled and frequent advice. She lectured Bart on making friends and staying active, checked that their wills and trust were up to date, then began planning her funeral. She wanted to be cremated, but she couldn't decide what to do with her ashes. She dismissed Bart's suggestion of a perpetual urn with a smiley face that could be handed down from generation to generation. Likewise dismissed his suggestion that her Burmese cat, a total pain in the ass, be cremated with her.

"You can do whatever you like. I won't be here, although I might visit you in the night if you off my cat." Bart knew she saw through him. She had seen him at too many funerals and sad movies.

He had watched Mary undergo chemo, go bald, buy a wig, ignore his suggestions that she sport a long-white ponytail with pink tips. In between the meals and the arrangements and the concern for Bart, Mary often sat in shadow. He would hold her, and she would cry. He would pretend to be strong. She said she welcomed the end, but he knew she didn't. She was scared and he could do nothing about it.

The kids visited, most of the grandchildren visited, her friends visited, and otherwise Mary led her "normal" life of family, friends, book group, discussion group, plays and concerts. That went on for most of two years until she no longer had strength. She was hospitalized briefly and sent home. And then she died. The cat got out two days later and never returned. Bart sometimes missed the cat, but soon thought better of it. For a while he just sat. Did nothing. Forgot about his nightly whisky and took long walks. It didn't help. And then? And then he couldn't remember. He knew time had passed.

Ch 19. A Walk in the Park

A short walk from the Jones "mini-ranch", one can find a large park covered with green grass, huge valley oaks and wandering pathways. The nearly 100-acre park offers play and relief from the heat of summer. At one end of the park, near a small lake, the Community Band plays outdoor concerts on Saturday nights, and the local Rotary Club sells barbeque for $10 a head. A green-lettered redwood sign informs visitors they enter "Horatio Ganesha Memorial Park".

Bart knew little about Horatio Ganesha. He had always intended to research the man but had never done it. From somewhere he remembered Ganesha was a Hindu god, god of wisdom maybe, and had something to do with elephants. This Horatio Ganesha probably had donated the land for the park, or maybe founded the city or won an Olympic medal. Bart only knew for certain that he was dead. He imagined Horatio as the son of a love match between a uniformed colonial general and an elegant Bengali princess dressed in gossamer and gold. Whatever. Horatio had succeeded in something.

Once a month, the San Sebastian Archery Club meets in Ganesha Park. Club members sport all types of bows from giant long bows to the latest multi-layered technical contraption. The archers are of two types: those fascinated by their equipment and those who like to shoot. Bart noticed the latter group shot about 10 arrows to the former's one. It was the same thing with bikes and cameras: some liked to ride and take pictures; others liked to fiddle with gears and lenses.

At the park's entrance, a large bulletin board lists archery activities for the week, including today's two o'clock archery discussion, "Dealing with Wind." Bart laughed. I'd love to give this lecture, all sorts of possibilities, but I think the club probably has something else in mind.

The archery club had roped off various sections of the park during their meets to avoid skewered pedestrians.

Skewered pedestrians oozed and smelled bad.

Originally a botanical garden, trees and flowers lined park trails and pathways, some still with their small green identification signs. The city kept the park clean, watered, and free of campers through the use of high-power sprinklers, citizen patrols, and prohibiting use from 10:00 pm to 6:00 am. These efforts kept the citizens happy and avoided the fate of some metro parks which residents could no longer safely use.

Bart saw her first. She ran without effort, immersed in another world. A testament to clean living? He had once been there, but when Mary died his need for fitness had left him. Now, watching Birdie run, he wanted to run again, run with her. Bart waved but she did not see him. He considered lying down in front of her, but that might be somewhat obvious. Then again, he might risk her jumping over him and suffer the pain of invisibility. But she smiled and stopped, bent down to pet Lily.

"Hi," she said. "Come, run with me. I know you've been a stone lately. I'll run slowly."

Having sat on his butt for the last two years, Bart would need a fast excuse to avoid puncturing his macho image. "What doesn't kill me makes me stronger?"

"Something like that. Are you into archery?"

Thoughts of shafts and quivers ran through Bart's mind not joining themselves in the witty semi-obscene combination he would have liked, so he said, "More like running away from the arrows. You know. Trying to save the dog."

"Of course," she said, and she started walking. "You know if you jogged every morning instead of walked, soon you could outrun most of the arrows or maybe get hit in the legs instead of the . . . ."

"Instead of the head," he said. "Maybe we could walk today before I begin running again." Birdie accepted, and for the next hour they walked the park trails talking of everything and nothing, identifying trees and pathways, commenting on local politics, playing with Lily. It seemed about five minutes to Bart.

Returning to the park entrance, they chatted for a moment while watching an archer struggle to separate a multilayered bow. The archer, a man in his 30s, said, "These things just want to stay together."

"Yeah," said Birdie, "I can understand that." She bent and rubbed Lily's head, looked at Bart for a few seconds. "I've really got to go," she said. Bart nodded, "I think I'll sit here and recover. Say hello to Higg for me." He watched her walk away, becoming but a small figure in the distance. Tired but happy, he relived the hour--the laughter, the smell of her clothing, the occasional touch.

What was he to Birdie? A friend? Someone to talk to, someone to listen? Would she be interested, seek him out if not for Higg? He could not know the answer to that question while Higg lived. And he was older than Birdie. She might end up with the last two years of a 12-year-old dog. He dismissed the thoughts. Enjoy the moment, the closeness, the walk in the park.

Higg awaited Birdie's return. He should have gone to the park. And done what? Sat on a bench? Yeah. Out of the house-- trees, people. Was he feeling sorry for himself? Probably. Maybe he just wanted to be done with it, whatever it was.

Birdie entered with a crash[She ran into doors; other people opened them. Physical objects--chairs, doors, tables-- were simply in the way. The softball catcher lived. He knew she had never sneaked out at night because she could not have gotten back in the house without alerting the neighborhood.

"I ran into Bart on the park path. He said to say hello. I tried to take him a pie but dropped it on the way over."

"Call him later and tell him where you dropped it. He can still have pie and you won't have to see the guy."

She studied her husband. "You feeling insecure?"

"Yeah"

"Higg, Bart's just a friend. You're my husband."

Ch 20. Mary Redux

A week later, Tuesday morning at 11:00, Bart walked around Dr. James' office to the waiting room. He knew it would be empty. Too bad. He could envision some great conversations with fellow patients. "Are you crazy or just want to talk about yourself?" Maybe, depending on whether the doctor had annoyed him the prior week, "I was afraid my sessions would be canceled when I heard about his indecent exposure charge." No such luck. So he sat and waited. Looked at all the empty glass-paned bookcases and thought of the book Nate had given him as a joke. Next appointment he would put *Bringing a Pet Pig into Your Home* on one of the shelves.

Finally, he was summoned. Nothing had changed. Clean desk. Tight black T-shirt. Smell of shower soap. Blue furniture. Little foreplay.

"How are you feeling?"

"I'm wonderful. Probably get better."

"As you know, I wanted to continue talking about Mary today. Discuss those feelings that may or may not be giving you trouble. Please, please think seriously about things today, be honest with your feelings.

"First question, if Mary were alive today, what advice would she be giving you?"

"She'd tell me to marry again."

"And?"

"Well, after considering my romantic prospects, I think I'd buy a life-sized blow-up doll, an expensive one with various "love" openings, though I fear it may stink at Jeopardy."

Dr. James frowned but otherwise did not react to Bart's attempt at humor. In a quiet voice he said, "I know this may be difficult for you, but it's in your interest. Talking about these feelings will help you, help you dig out those things that got you here in the first place."

Bart felt like he did when he had passed a note in third grade and got caught. "You're right, and I apologize. It's a difficult subject for me, a difficult subject to talk about. Let's go on." He looked at the clock on the wall. He had 50 minutes to go.

"She would want me to date, remarry, start a new life."

"And are you doing these things?"

"I'm not sure I want to do them."

"Do you stay home now more than you did while Mary lived?"

Stay at home. Bart saw his wife in her blue bathrobe, sleepy, making breakfast. For several seconds he said nothing. "Sure, but I'm also several years older. Mary generated many of our outings—like performances and plays. And many of the things we did were with couples. I'm now the odd man out. Three's a crowd.

"Doctor, I loved my wife; I think about her every day. She was my best friend; someone I could trust." Bart looked away, avoided the doctor's constant stare. "Sometimes. . . sometimes during the last months. . . I felt she took more care of me than I did of her. She focused on what would happen to me after she was gone. Saw me as the vulnerable one, the one in danger. Maybe that was her defense. And I really could do nothing to help her." Bart's speech became difficult, fragmented. He saw again that painful year, saw Mary, felt her struggle. "She's still with me."

Dr. James said, "I realize this conversation must be difficult for you. I can't begin to imagine what you went through. I'm sure you did everything possible."

"I'd like to believe that. But even when I understood things, understood why she behaved as she did, I didn't always act as I should have. Behind her activity, her concern for me, she was scared. And she struck out, attacked me."

"Struck out at you?"

He could still see her when the darkness took her. She would change, physically change. Her skin, her flesh, would lose its support, its structure, turn grey and dark. She became cruel and unforgiving, and he became a match to gasoline.

He looked up. "It was unfair. The disease tortured her and not me, and I think that—the unfairness of it all—caused her to strike out, to attack me because I did not physically suffer. When the blackness seized her, it didn't matter what I said or did."

Lost in thought, he remembered the Sunday morning when he had decorated their dining room table with red roses from their garden. Diffused sunlight had lit the room and he could still smell the toast and the ripe strawberries. While she had slept, he had made breakfast hoping the food would cheer her. But she sat through breakfast moving her food around and did not talk. After cleaning up, he remembered saying, "Lily hasn't been out yet. I'm going to take her for a short walk." She became ugly. "All you think about is that fucking dog. You're so self-centered. I may not be here when you get back, as if you care."

Bart leaned back in his chair, reliving this special Sunday morning. His hamstring hurt and he wanted this session to end.

"Bart," said Dr. James, "Are you still with me?'

"Sorry, I tuned out."

"Memories?"

"Yeah. Was remembering a blowup which ended with her threatening to leave. No good deed goes unpunished, I guess."

"And did she leave?"

"No."

"What did you do when there was a blowup?"

"Hung out. Waited for the storm to pass. It rarely lasted. Usually the real Mary returned in a few hours. I wasn't perfect.

When she started yelling abuse, I kept my cool or tried to, but there were times when I lost it, got in her face and shouted back at her even though I knew she was just acting out—acting out like a little kid who hadn't got enough sleep. I was the adult and needed to act as an adult.

"Later she would apologize, beg forgiveness. "

"Did you forgive her? Have you forgiven her? "

"Nothing to forgive. She was sick and dying."

"Was her anger toward you sometimes justified?"

"Yes, in the sense that I often did not respond or comfort her in the way she would have liked. But I didn't know. I did what I thought was best."

"But you feel guilty?"

"Yeah, but I'm not sure about what. It's probably the guilt I was born with."

"Adam and Eve?"

"No, Kafka."

Bart's response stopped the doctor who, for a moment, lost his train of thought.

"If you could relive that last six months, what would you have done differently?"

"Don't know really. As it was, I talked with Hospice, sought advice from her doctors. Been another person, I suppose. The anger was not that frequent, and I believe it was frustration, her inability to control things. She struck out at the hopelessness of the situation. It was a time to have faith, but Mary, despite her holy name, did not believe."

"Have you forgiven yourself?"

Bart got up and took a bottle of water from the doctor's drink cooler. After a minute or two, he returned to his chair.

"Have I forgiven myself? No, not really. I made mistakes."

"And then you sheltered in place."

"Let's be honest. Mary had died. A forty-year marriage had come to an end. The following months were exhausting with well-wishers, family, ceremonies, ashes and all that. Once everyone left and we were done with the protocol, the house was blessedly quiet for a while. I was happy to stay at home, at least until I met you, Doc." Bart winked.

"And your neighbor."

"Yes. And my neighbor. One of my neighbors. I've got several other neighbors you wouldn't want to meet. The enclosure to the south of my house harbors the gossip of the ages. "Nosey" does not begin to describe her. She would put cameras and sound equipment in your toilet if you'd let her. On the other side lives Higg, the husband of the neighbor I like. I'm convinced Higg is 'on the spectrum' and converses only because his mommy told him it was the right thing to do. Unfortunately, she never told him about dialogue, nor did she issue him an off button."

"Tell me about Mrs. Higgins."

"The drone's wife. A genuinely nice person. My piano teacher. She also feeds me from time to time. Pies with golden crusts and crunchy sugar. I like her a lot."

"But she's married?"

"Yes, currently married to the drone, but maybe not for long."

"You're gonna take her away from him?"

"No, I thought I'd tie him in front of a mirror and let him bore himself to death." Bart was not liking this conversation. "No. Higg may not be with us much longer. His only kidney is diseased and failing. Because of his age and medical history, he cannot get a transplant—though I could probably save his sorry ass with one of my kidneys. Or not. Think I'll just do whatever you decide, Doc."

The doctor said nothing, leaned back in his chair and continued with his usual patient and expectant stare. This was a game for control and Bart could play it as well. But Dr. James, despite his long hair and tight T-shirts, was giving his best professional effort, and Bart believed he cared. Finally Bart said, "Well?"

"Sure, go for it. I'll call the hospital and see if we can get you in this afternoon."

"Or, I can do nothing," said Bart, "and get the girl.

"Is there pressure on you from Mrs. Higgins?"

"No. She doesn't know my thoughts or that I could donate. And there are multiple questions and possibilities. Do I risk my life to save Marvin Higgins, a person I don't particularly like? I have done that before. If we weren't talking about hospitals and cutting, of course, the decision would be easier. That's not to say I would do it. If I do it and it succeeds, I lose the girl. If I do nothing, the gate is open. But I like the idea of giving to someone who has no power. It's selfless, noble. Will I have done Mrs. Higgins a favor? Would she be better off with someone else?" Bart shrugged his shoulders.

"You said you've risked your life for someone you didn't particularly like."

"Yes, in the Marine Corps. During training, our helicopter crashed and caught fire. I went back into the crash to pull out one of the biggest jerks in the unit.

"How is saving Higg any different from saving a fellow Marine?"

"My fellow Marines were my brothers. My life depended on them; theirs on me. Marines fight for the good of our country, and most of the time they don't get the credit they deserve. Aside from the brotherhood, society values Marines and saving a Marine benefits society. I'm not sure society benefits by saving Higg, and he certainly isn't my brother."

"But Mrs. Higgins does."

"I'd like to think so. Certainly she cares for him, owes him really. I don't think there's any romance. There's just a lady doing her duty. And we're assuming the operation succeeds, I live, Higg lives, the kidney is not rejected and does not become diseased. We're assuming Mrs. Higgins wants to continue her life with Higg, that she wouldn't welcome a new life. Whole lot of assumptions.

"And you? Would rebirth do you well? A new life?"

Bart pictured the little oak on the dry field fluttering its green flags. The odds were against it. "I can't imagine starting anew at my age. The mere thought of it makes me tired."

"But you could live another 20 years, maybe longer."

"That's what makes me tired."

The clock on the wall showed11:07. The doctor said, "I'm afraid we're out of time. I'm sorry. We'll continue this next week."

Bart nodded. Got his coat and went out the back door. He felt suddenly alone. Maybe Mary had felt this way. He retreated to his truck. It was almost out of gas, but he drove straight home.

He still felt guilty and was not sure why. He had given Mary everything he had to give. Dr. James asked him about guilt, but then he let it drop. And donating a kidney? Bart locked the truck doors. He would not die from a transplant.

Ch 21. Grocery

Grocery stores always reminded Bart of playing Bach on the piano. The food, like the notes matter, but location, like fingering, is everything. Based on this week's politics, pinto beans are now found with tortillas and poblano chilis, kidney beans with canned green beans. Really? And fresh tomatoes —well he didn't like fresh tomatoes, so they could put them wherever they wanted. But assuming you did need to find them, you wouldn't find them with tomato sauce, or tomato paste, or ketchup. Thankfully, these organizational zealots had yet to find spices. Bart foresaw a future diaspora where spices would be separated by country of origin or scattered throughout the store based on what you were trying to cook: cumin in a Mexican food section, basil in an Italian food section, cardamom with candy, dill with Nordic foods. Salt, he imagined, would cause severe ethnic conflict.

In his search, Bart found fresh eggs in an upright column located across an aisle from last week's location. He confessed these frequent changes worked. He was forced to tour the entire store almost every week to find the same foods.

As Bart exited the cereal aisle, a small child of indeterminant age embraced him at Mach 5, knocking him back about a foot and bringing the kid to an abrupt and unceremonious halt.

"Hi," said Bart. "You OK?"

The kid, red-faced and out of breath, looked up at Bart with a mixture of anger and guilt. As the child recoiled, he backed into his father, who, evidently, had given chase from peanut butter to the egg rack.

"Hi, Bart," said Dr. James looking startled, "I see you and Miles have met."

"I thought for a moment he was going to molest me, but he was just eager to show me where they had relocated the eggs.

I think he's going to be a future linebacker like his dad."

James frowned at Miles. "What did we talk about?"

"Not running in the store," Miles said.

"Miles, this is Mr. Jones, a friend of mine. He's a lawyer so you might not want to run into him again."

"Don't let him scare you. I've only eaten one child this week, and he didn't feel a thing."

"Really?"

"No, not really."

Dr. James looked back at his cart and then at Bart. "So, is this your weekly outing?"

"Yeah, I was shopping for a bowling ball, but they've moved them again. Where's Momma?"

The doctor smiled. "Miles and I are out and about today. Momma and Emma, Miles' sister, went to a baby shower."

"You weren't invited?"

"No, thankfully." Dr. James asked Miles to retrieve the shopping cart. "Anything going on with you?"

Before Bart could answer, an elderly shopper, excusing herself, maneuvered her cart through the aisle. When she had passed, Bart said, "Not much. Fear of death, guilt, search for meaning. No, just trying to find Twinkies to go along with my beer."

Miles reappeared, pushing the doctor's shopping cart, which sported potato chips, Velveeta cheese, Fruit Loops, whole milk, Tatter Tots and ice cream. Bart immediately saw Mary and could hear her reaction. From the start of their relationship, she had mandated healthy eating. And so he had spent his entire married life eating vegetables and whole grains with little or no salt, and red meat once every winter solstice. Mary did not consider potatoes a vegetable and thought ice cream the equivalent of lard. She said, with some truth, Bart's basic food groups were salt, sugar and grease. Feeling put-upon and deprived, Bart would eat hamburgers at every rare opportunity. However, over the many years, Mary's nutrition had had an effect, and he now saved hamburger consumption for special occasions, like when he wanted a hamburger, or to react to someone eating kale or discussing gas from cattle.

"Comfort food?" said Bart.

The doctor frowned. "Doesn't look too healthy, does it? Although I do work out every morning." He started to move on.

"Yeah, but if you put water in your gas tank, your engine's not going to get you down the road too well. And," said Bart, "how is a healthy body different from a healthy mind?"

"Good and evil go together I guess. I've had courses in nutrition, but I really can't stand most green stuff." The doctor again started moving. Miles had disappeared.

"So, like Ovid (and Bart Jones), you see and approve the good, but follow the evil."

"I've got to go," said James who was biting his lower lip. "God knows what Miles is up to."

Standing aside Bart said, "How can you be my role model when you fill your body with junk? You have hidden the true Anthony James behind tight T-shirts and exercise equipment. You're no different from Bart Jones."

James stared at Bart and then relaxed, seemingly forgetting about Miles for the moment. "Wow," he said, "how did that make you feel?"

"Doesn't change anything, "said Bart. "That you're a real person like the rest of us, doesn't take away from your professional knowledge and training—although it's a bit hypocritical to counsel feelings when, with all the crap you're eating, you don't feel for yourself."

Dr. James grimaced and slowly nodded his head. He started moving again. "I think I'll wander over to the deli section and commune with my fellow rotisserie chickens."

"Say 'hello' for me. I've rotated with the best of them." He stopped the doctor with his hand. "I think you're doing a good job with me and with showing me what's under the rock. And I'm glad you eat potato chips. If you were perfect, I'd be waiting for an ascension or, more likely, a hatchet murder. See you Tuesday."

"It may be Tuesday before I can find Miles."

Bart watched the doctor go and stood thinking about Tuesday until wakened by the "Excuse me, excuse me" of an impatient shopper. Bart wheeled his cart from the aisle. He saw only a multitude of shoppers, scurrying like beetles around the store. Whatever he had wanted had left him.

Ch 22. Morning T

Bart walked on streets this morning; his usual trails turned to mud by the wet fog. He had traveled but a short distance, not yet emptied Lily, when he found himself face-to-face with Granny T. ("Heard you're seeing Dr. James. Is everything all right?" "No, just a bad case of ED., Gladys. It clips my wings.") She had marched off in her usual snoot.

After his recent "donation discussion" with Dr. James, Bart was reluctant to go next door and sit with Birdie at the piano. She would know something had changed. But the lesson proceeded normally, although Birdie seemed at times to be elsewhere. How on earth did he get involved in all this? Mary, you fox, is this your doing?

He had been a bit lonely, but happy, peaceful. Had finally got a chance to look out the window, see the sunshine on the oaks and an occasional deer. The deer ate the plump buds of his roses, ate them one second before they bloomed. Frustrating, but frequent in a dry year. Couldn't blame them. Rose buds probably contained some needed vitamin.

And now? And now what, thought Bart? The kids disapprove of my lack of activity, want me warehoused with people of my advanced age and passé beliefs. Birdie's my close friend, but might prefer a kidney. Dr. James. . . Dr. James has helped, at least helped me see the real Bart. But I'm not sure I agree with the Bart that Dr. James is wanting. Well, he said to himself, so what? You can all want to your heart's content. At the end of the day, I'm still the chairman of Bart, Inc..

The fog abating, the morning transformed slowly into blue sky—no doubt "cerulean" thought Bart with a smile. But his smile soon faded, dimmed by the thought of a transplant. It scared him. Worth the risk to save Higg? Probably not. Aside from his lack of use for Higg, Higg had a history of cancer and might not survive in any case. Right thing for Birdie? She would want to save Higg, but Bart thought she would be better off without him. Yet he felt he should donate. Felt it was the right thing to do. What about Sophie and Nate? This wasn't about them. Still the idea scared him. He would call Sophie. Sophie would say, "Don't do it." She would give him an out, an excuse.

Bart got up from his overstuffed chair, went into his bedroom in search of his cell phone. In the process, he knocked over his coffee cup and spent the next 15 minutes on his hands and knees getting brown out of the carpet. Carpet clean, he discovered the phone in his pocket and called Sophie.

◆ ◆ ◆

"Dad, you don't even like this guy. And think of your grandchildren and their grandfather. You had no grandparents; how did that work out for you?"

"I had grandparents, for a little while at least. Fond memories in fact. Granddad Jones carried a one-gallon coffee can around with him as a portable spittoon for his chew. Nice guy. He taught me tolerance as I watched him eat soup at the kitchen table. A large spit string followed every spoonful to his mouth. To my credit I never puked. He was frail. Weighed maybe 140 pounds. Basically, he lived on the couch and slept. Grandmother Jones died when I was three.

"On the other side of the family, the Orleans side, Grandpa — 'Bonpapa' as he was called--died before I was born. I thought Grand-mère scary and judgmental, although I didn't use the word, 'judgmental' then. She did say nice things to me, but always with a stern face. Mom said she was sick and wasn't herself. She died when I was seven.

"Both of them, Grandad Jones and Grand-mère Orleans lived in New Mexico and Texas, so I saw them only a week or so per year. Your kids are 3000 miles away. I doubt my absence would have any significant effect on their lives. One less present at Christmas and birthday."

"Maybe, but it would have a significant effect on my life and Nate's as well."

"Of course, but it could be for the better—that is, if I don't leave my estate to The Society for the Benefit Indigent Lawyers. Besides, I don't plan on dying. Can't get the girl, any girl, if I die."

"So Dad, skip the donation and get the girl. Listen, you've got 20 years ahead of you. Do you really want to cut it short?"

"I don't think I'll be cutting it short."

"Have you talked with Nate?

"Not yet, but I know what he'd tell me. He'd tell me it's my body and I can do whatever I want with it."

Sophie suggested Bart take a break, get out of the house. Take a cruise; meet people, take some time to think.

He liked the idea of a cruise. He could eat his way around the world, away from shrinks, children and neighbors, visit new and exciting places. Or, he could just walk out, cancel the shrink sessions, wish Birdie good luck. He'd paid his dues. Spent his life helping people. No. Birdie and Dr. James and Higg would be in his head every single day. He should donate. It's resolution.

Ch 23. ER

Higg leaned against the passenger door while Birdie focused on driving Higg's pickup. She normally drove a small sporty Miata, but Higg, at present, could not get up and out of it, so she drove his truck. Easier to step up and get down than get down and climb up. Birdie convinced herself long ago she could do anything but was uneasy as she steered the beast through traffic. It's like blocking home plate. They'll avoid me, and if they don't, I'll win.

Most of the time she loved a summer night with its breezes and cool. The dark hid the day, silenced it, gave her permission to dream. But tonight, left alone with her thoughts, the lonely drive revealed feelings about Higg, about Bart, about a marriage still serving as a placeholder. After college she had put her life on hold--and left it there.

Up ahead a green freeway sign, an illuminated sentinel in the darkness: "St. Stephen's Hospital, 5 miles." With night surrounding, she had little sense of speed. Doing 85 she slowed down, not wanting to roll over or be pulled over. She hoped she would not wait long tonight, hoped she would not see flashing lights and a full ER.

Higg continued leaning against the passenger door and said little. On automatic pilot in the darkness, Birdie dreamed of Bart's warm kitchen. I love taking him apple pie with cinnamon, love his smile, love his voice. She woke with a start. She had struck an animal—a dog, a coyote—she didn't know what. She could not see in the darkness. There was no noise, just the dual thump of tires, the feeling of helplessness. Shaken, she slowed but did not stop.

Higg still lay against the passenger door. What kind of person takes her husband to the hospital while driving and dreaming of another man? She forced herself to talk, talk about anything to keep up his spirits, and her own. "We'll be there soon, assuming I don't kill anything else." She talked about driving his big truck, said she was going to make him drive the Miata next time they went out. Said Higg had to start eating again or she'd have to find other neighbors to give food to, and she wasn't keen on hanging with Gladys Tharp.

"You like Bart", he said with an edge in his voice. "He'll be with you when I'm gone."

"You're not going anywhere. We'll find a donor. Maybe we can talk Bart into it." But she knew she would not ask Bart, did not want to ask Bart.

"Fat chance of that. I'm not Bart's favorite, but I suppose you could persuade him."

"Higg, Bart's just a neighbor. He's next door. I don't have to walk half a mile to offload a pie." True enough. But there was more to it. Often she fled the monotony of Higg, for the warmth and gratitude of Bart. Too often. He was there, he listened. There had never been more than conversation, talk. Nevertheless, if only in thought and for a time, she could forget Higg, look at a life that might have been. But she would do the right thing for Higg. She always had.

A large white awning covered the brightly lit entrance to the St. Stephen's Emergency Room. There were no ambulances tonight, so Higg might get immediate attention. She parked close and helped Higg to the pedestrian entrance. As they walked together, she could smell the jasmine so fragrant in the evening air. She knew machinery noise and the antiseptic smell of modern medicine would soon replace it.

They were out of the hospital in two hours, something of a record. The nurse had asked Birdie to stay in the waiting room. She normally went with Higg during dialysis, but tonight was not normal. Higg had just had dialysis. The nurse, Isabel, told her the cafeteria still was open if Birdie wanted something to eat or drink. Had she been able to buy wine, she might have gone. As to food, desiccated turkey on cardboard did not appeal.

After the procedure, Dr. Marks came to the lobby and sat beside Birdie. The doctor had been Higg's urologist for some time and had almost become a friend of the family. It was sheer luck he was on call this evening.

"I wanted to talk with you before we brought Higg out." He paused, seemed to gather himself. "I'd like to tell you things have not changed, but they have, and they have not changed for the better." Birdie watched him, feeling only the emptiness of the huge lobby. "This evening he was exhausted and weak. I don't think he will live long without a transplant. And Birdie, I'm afraid something else may be going on. It may be nothing, but I suggest he see his oncologist as soon as possible."

They brought him out in a wheelchair. When he saw Birdie he half smiled. Covered in his rumpled grey canvas jacket, he looked as if he were falling in on himself, like the evil lord in a movie who vanishes into a pile of clothing. No, not really, more like an old white-muzzled golden retriever still with love and hope in his eyes.

"Mrs. Higgins? Is everything all right?" She had not seen the nurse nor realize she had stopped moving. Higg looked up at her, watched her. "Yes, thank you. It's been a difficult evening." As she pushed Higg's wheelchair toward the large entry she felt uneasy, but smiled and stroked Higg's head. A new life must wait.

Ch 24. Entourage

Bart puttered around the house going from room to room. When he could see—daylight would have guaranteed a more thorough cleaning—he straightened pictures and dusted. He should have done this during the day and not at 10:00 at night. But Nate had called earlier and would arrive with a companion around noon tomorrow. He wanted at least to appear in control.

Who would it be this time? Rich, in suede, with understated gold jewelry and tipped hair? Or plump with bib overalls and bad teeth? Nate chose mates like he sampled chocolates: sometimes a cherry center, sometimes a chew, sometimes a nut. If he didn't like what he bit, he put it back in the box. His selections were always interesting. Bart remembered Martha, a biker chick with language so imaginatively offensive, that Bart found himself convulsed in laughter. She could kill or change any subject simply by opening her mouth. Dr. James would say Bart used humor in the same way—as a shield to protect the core.

And then there was the elegant Ms. Rose. Ms. Rose looked upon San Sebastian, with its abundant dirt roads, as West Africa and feared pestilence and disease in anything not paved. Gated and cloistered, she had defenses like Bart and biker chick. Maybe I'm just like everyone else, thought Bart. Maybe there are no "open" people.

With Nate there were always more chocolates. Bart hoped at some point Nate might find one he liked and put away the box. Someone like Mary maybe, someone who would put some stability in his life.

The black Mercedes Van pulled up around 3:00 in the afternoon, disgorged Nate, two women, and enough luggage for a tour group. Although the giant car had no baggage-claim sign, it might have had a carousel inside. Alerted by Lily, Bart stood in the shade of his doorway, watching the disembarkation. Nate often traveled with a woman companion. These "companions," never the same, embraced the full spectrum of human looks and behavior. Nate had yet to travel with men, but maybe men were the next step in his romantic evolution. But two women? Two at once? Or maybe one and a spare? If this were a competition for Nate, they would be disappointed—not because Nate wasn't rich and interesting, but because he lived his work and would disappear for weeks at a time. They would soon find he had another mistress.

"Sorry for the late arrival," said Nate. "Got a late start."

"Looks like you brought all of Portola Valley with you."

"Yeah, it does, doesn't it. Help me get this stuff inside and I'll introduce you to Toni and Betty."

"You all gonna stay in one room?"

"Not sure I'm ready for that." Nate winked. "Too much luggage."

Nate's two "dates", Toni and Betty, each had three suitcases and miscellaneous other stuff packed in shopping bags. Toni, tanned, with full figure and half-naked in a yellow miniskirt and halter top, rapidly chewed at least three pieces of Juicy Fruit. She reminded Bart of an open-mouthed popcorn popper with giggles, except popcorn smelled a whole lot better. No doubt she signs her name with a smiley face over the "i", that is, if she can write at all. Sure glad I spent all that money on Nate at Stanford and Berkeley. Well maybe it's not about the mind. Comfort food, perhaps. Something soft and warm in the night. But what do you do with her during the day? Who do you talk to?

And then there was Betty, the friend. Tall, weathered, wizened, stoic--she could be a member of the Joad family. She made little noise and had dark tired eyes that had seen everything.

"Nice digs," said Toni. "You could fit my apartment into your kitchen." She took her gum out of her mouth and looked around for a place to put it. Fearing a giant wad underneath his dining room table, Bart found a tissue and rescued her. She then proceeded to inspect the house as if she were a real estate agent opening cupboards, drawers, closets."

"My underwear drawer is down the hall," said Bart.

Toni giggled. "Ooh sorry."

Nate, loving the theatre of the situation, kept a straight face.

Betty, meanwhile, organized and transported luggage to the various assigned rooms.

Shaking his head in astonishment, Bart said, "What's the deal? Do you sleep with one and talk to the other?"

"We have an event in Santa Barbara tomorrow. Betty, you talked with Betty over the phone, coordinated this event and will see all the proper backsides scratched and questions answered. She will insure we maneuver those who must be maneuvered. Betty runs the operation when I'm not around. Actually, she runs the operation when I am around.

"Toni provides entertainment and distracts people from what is really happening. To be effective, they can't know they're being manipulated. They can suspect it, but they can't know it. So Toni obfuscates, pleases, keeps everything from getting too real. Toni has a BFA in theatre from Northwestern and an MFA from USC. She also has a passle of acting roles to her credit. We want our event remembered; stuck in our client's minds. Not just another "group grope". Toni plays whatever role we ask of her, from bimbo to sophisticated lady. Thus, all the luggage. So there you are, the chameleon and the anchor. I'm just along for the ride."

"Manipulation? I thought you were in public relations. What exactly do you do?"

"We persuade, attempt to convince decision makers to a client's position. Public relations with a focus. But usually more involved than just issues--staging, optics, personal gain, whatever works."

Yeah, whatever works thought Bart, whatever works to persuade. Whatever works in the legal profession gets you a disciplinary hearing before the state bar. Sure, legal persuasion is the goal. And staging and optics help. But there is one gigantic difference: a trial has rules.

◆ ◆ ◆

After a night at Casa Jones—not a great night for Nate, he slept on the Hide-a-Bed—the foursome lunched at the Forge, a "new age" restaurant. The Forge had been a Mary favorite. Mary believed "natural" food—massaged kale and other weed-like concoctions--contributed to one's health and well-being. Bart thought the food appealed primarily to rabbits, though he was unsure a rabbit would eat kale. Fortunately, the restaurant offered an alternative menu which allowed Bart his preferred dead animal flesh.

The foursome sat around what looked like a thick varnished picnic table made of un-planed tree. Toni had transformed during the night and now resembled an executive on her day off. White blouse, grey slacks, comfortable black shoes. No gum, subdued pastel lipstick, and maybe a hint of eyeshadow. Betty still looked like a member of the Joad family.

"What's good?" said Toni.

"I'm not the one to ask," said Bart. "I usually eat at the top of the food chain, although I've yet to try long pork."

Toni pursed her lips. "Maybe you should move to Papua New Guinea. You could put a bone in your nose and eat tourists, and then, after you lost your bone," she winked, "you could write a novel about losing your identity."

"I think I've already lost that. Speaking of loss of identity, what happened to Toni with her mini skirt and Juicy Fruit? I was becoming quite fond of her."

"It's called rehearsing. I wanted to remain in character for a while. We have an event this coming week and when needed, I will distract and entertain. But here today I'm off stage, plain old Antonia in the real world. I don't have be Toni the bimbo until Wednesday, so I get a little rest. But don't get me wrong, I love this job. These gigs pay well and are spaced so I can pursue legitimate theatre. I did both The Glass Menagerie and King Lear last year as well as appearing at the local melodrama. And these gig characters are more fun than work, but I'll admit I don't think too hard about whatever cockamamy goal we're after."

Before Bart could respond, a waiter appeared large alongside the table and interrupted the conversation. Said, "My name is Bruce and I'll be serving you today." He recited the specials including the locality where each ingredient had been grown and harvested. He asked if we were ready to order. Betty had to be pulled back to life from the weekend addition of the Wall Street Journal and Nate from his cell phone. After several minutes, Nate, Toni and Betty ordered the house salad with kale and sea scallops; Bart ordered a rare hamburger.

Looking around the table, Bart felt like a stranger. The people around him were not real and would change in a week or so. Toni the bimbo would morph into Antonia the college professor. His son with his dark sport coat, open white shirt, and carefully tended two-day beard would embrace another belief.

Nate, seemingly aware of his dad's unease, said, "I'm the same Nate, Dad. But in our business, appearance is the only reality, or, if you prefer, 'All is not what it seems.'"

"What happens if you strongly disagree with the position you're taking?"

"We convince people to support or oppose a way of thinking. Whether that way is right or wrong is not our concern. Obviously we must analyze a position and its various outcomes. We have to do that in order to see what we must do to get people to come around. But we don't judge. The merit of the client's position, its effects on other people, do not concern us. We only have one client, and our job is to persuade."

Bart felt a horror. "So I could hire your firm to advocate euthanasia of the mentally ill?"

"No, we left all that behind in 1945. We wouldn't advocate murder, or anything illegal for that matter. But we might agree to change views on mandatory hospitalization, either pro or con.   Our client normally would be some public agency or advocacy group. And again, whether what they wanted was in the best interests of the mentally ill, would not be our concern. And realize, Dad, advocates believe their ideas righteous or beneficial to someone.

Bart looked unconvinced.

"Dad, we don't do illegal things. We persuade and educate; we do not force or extort. And we don't judge. We focus solely on accomplishing what the client wants. "

Nate's visit disturbed Bart.   Nate's callousness, his disregard for the propriety or damage his "persuasion" might cause, his singular focus. Actions in a vacuum thought Bart. Like persuading people to disregard vehicle maintenance to benefit towing companies.

Outside, Mr. Tharp burned pine needles in his fire pit. Four-foot flames in the heat and dry of summer. God, hope he watches the fire. Johnny, please keep your neighbor in mind. I've no desire to become a taco chip.

Nate and his acting cast left after making multiple trips to their Mercedes Van with bags, duffels, and boxes all color coded with red stripes and white squares. Most stenciled with "KG" for "Knowledge Group". Both women, now dressed down for moving in jeans and T-shirts, smelled faintly of perfume. A clean smell thought Bart.

As the group packed to leave, Bart could see Granny T watching intently from a side window. She had not dressed yet, wearing only a faded red bathrobe. He waved but got no response.

"Thanks, Dad. Sorry I couldn't have hooked you up with either Toni or Betty."

"Yeah, too bad. I planned on acting out my wildest fantasy with Toni--you know, the one where I buy a new set of canning jars. And, of course, I expected Betty to analyze my stock portfolio. Maybe next time. What's today's mission?"

"Public agency. What we call a specialty agency. Employs people, but no longer has a purpose. It was originally created for county asbestos abatement, but there's no longer any asbestos to abate. With luck we will persuade the county supervisors to keep funding the agency—keep the spigot flowing."

"And that doesn't bother you—the funding of a useless agency."

"Well it's something I have to deal with, because we've got to persuade supervisors the agency is useful. Maybe they employ 15 people, support 60 family members. Maybe their mission can be shifted to poison oak abatement. But our client is the public agency, not the taxpayers, not the employees, not the public. If continuing this agency works to their detriment, so be it. These groups are not our client."

Nate got into his van and left with his entourage. Bart did not see him off.

Dr. James always sat to the side of Bart or at least diagonally across from him. Same thing as in Bart's office where he did not want to oppose a client. This morning Bart wanted to talk about Nate, not about defensive humor or lack of empathy for the feelings of others. He knew the doctor would quickly turn the conversation. That was the doctor's job, but Bart now paid the freight. So, after the "How are you feeling?" conversation, Bart told Dr. James he wanted to ask the doctor some questions, not personal questions, but questions. James raised open hands, said "Shoot".

Leaning toward the doctor, Bart said, "Do you consider public relations and advertising ethical?"

The doctor thought for a moment. "Usually, I guess, because most people know what advertisers are trying to do."

"What about the subtle stuff? For example, where you have a choice of walkways, you walk to the right because the architect made the right walkway wider than the left walkway. Or, where a shop pumps cinnamon smell into the air a block before you reach the pastry shop. Or the "Buy Acme Rice" that pops up for a microsecond in a movie or a TV show? Is this manipulation good or bad?"

" Depends. Advertising doesn't bother me because I know they're trying to persuade me. Subliminal messages—the fraction of a second on the TV—bothers me, I think, because I don't know it's happening--although I've read it doesn't work. But with normal advertising the choice is mine, and I would like to think I would make a decision based upon my own interests. Advertising would bother me if it controlled me, made it so I couldn't avoid doing what they wanted." Dr. James stared sidelong at Bart. "What's on your mind?"

"My son, Nate, manipulates behavior, manipulates it with success. He makes lots of money. Agencies, companies hire him to persuade influential people and decision makers to certain views: money views, policy views, legislative views. Nate works to achieve what his client wants. He does not judge. As long as the client's goal wouldn't violate some law, he doesn't concern himself if it would be good, bad, or hurt thousands."

"How is that different from a political ad or a lawyer who defends a murderer and returns the person to the street? Or what about writing a will favoring one child over the rest of the family?"

"The legislature designed criminal laws to reach a just result—or at least as just as reasonably could be expected. A prosecutor presents evidence against an accused murderer. A defense attorney defends the accused. The accused goes to jail if the evidence convinces a jury that the accused committed the crime. The law focuses on reaching a just and fair outcome, with each side represented by a lawyer. Nate doesn't concern himself with a just and fair outcome, he concerns himself with giving the client what the client wants, whether good or bad.

"With respect to a will, a good lawyer will point out that favoring one child over another, even with the best of intentions, can destroy the future relationship between these children. For example, say parents have a son who has done nothing with his life and lives hand-to-mouth; they have a daughter who has worked hard and become a neurosurgeon. If parents leave their estate to the son because he doesn't have much, the daughter will most often think the unequal result unfair. Why should she be punished for working hard and he be rewarded for doing nothing?

"Legally, the lawyer must do what the client wants or withdraw. At the same time the lawyer has an ethical duty to do what's in the best interests of the client, and would have a duty to tell the client that his unequal division might destroy the relationship between brother and sister. But the lawyer, a good lawyer, will be concerned with what's good for the client and the client's family. Do the clients want the son to get the money if they might break up the family relationship between son and daughter? Nate tries to achieve his client's goal, whether its righteous or may damage a lot of people."

The doctor said, "So if I understand you, you have rules you must follow, and your rules say you do what the client wants as long as it's legal."

"I must also do what's in the best interest of the client."

"OK, but If you don't like what the client wants, you can either hold your nose and do it, or withdraw. And under these rules a murderer might walk, and a client's family get disinherited. And, at the end of the day. . . " The doctor tossed his notebook on his desk and leaned back in his chair. ". . . you must follow the wishes of your client.

The doctor looked Bart in the eye. "How are you any different from Nate? Like Nate, you focused on your client and did what was in the best interests of that client. Yes, you had rules to fall back on, but rules permitting, you might still throw the daughter under the bus. And you might not like it, but you couldn't worry about it because you had to do what the client wanted. The children were not your clients."

Bart reddened, "I didn't conduct charades with paid actors, and I discussed the likely outcome of proposed actions. For example, giving a child from a former marriage control over a trust for the client's current spouse, can end in conflict and legal action despite the kid's outspoken "love and affection" for the stepmother. Many children of a first marriage will squash their stepmother at the first opportunity. The converse also is true. I counseled clients against doing something that would hurt the client or the client's family."

The doctor said nothing, merely looked at the high window where the summer sunshine had melted the fog and begun to heat the room. The light identified all of the room's features and made it less a place of refuge.

Bart said, "Surely you see the difference between

counseling a client on the likely outcome of a proposed action and simply following the client's wishes if legal."

"And you think Nate doesn't consider the likely outcome?"

"Sure, whether he can achieve it, not whether it has merit."

"But, like Nate, you did what you client wanted, and, like Nate, you did not concern yourself with people not your clients."

Bart looked at the doctor in disbelief. "Have you listened to what I've said?" Bart heard the edge in his voice but did not care. "I had to concern myself with the effect of what a client wanted to do, the collateral damage if you will. I had to concern myself with how a proposed estate plan would affect the client's family and children, even though they were not my clients. Yes, I limited my concern, my empathy, to my clients. But that's a different issue, an issue of self-preservation. I'm not my brother's keeper, not now, not then. In my legal practice, I couldn't concern myself with everyone, just as you can't concern yourself with the mental health of Gladys Tharp or my daughter, Sophie. Nate achieves outcomes; he does not judge their merit. Bart achieved outcomes after discussion of their merits with his clients. But none of them, neither Bart nor Nate nor Dr. James is big enough to deal with the problems of clients and also of everyone else."

"What about Billy?"

"Oh, come on," said Bart, "I understood Billy and knew where he was coming from. You understand Gladys Tharp and see her as a lonely old lady whose life has passed her by. Neither are our clients or patients. We can recognize their pain but don't have to share it. Maybe you do. I'm not that big a person." Bart felt the still life of the small room: two men at a desk, one young, one with grey hair, a walnut desk, a notebook, some exercise equipment, a window with filtered light.

The doctor sat with crossed arms and did not look at Bart.

"You're upset about Nate, yet he's not your client."

"I'm upset about Nate because he's my son."

Ch 25. BBQ

This Saturday, as a thank you for their kindness, and assuage his feeling of guilt, Bart had invited Mr. and Mrs. Higgins to join him for barbeque and band concert in Ganesha Park. At the park one paid first, then stood in line to reach the barbeque pit for a choice of chicken or tri-tip. The line often was long and much of it unshaded. Standing in line, Bart listened to Higg while Birdie saved them spaces at one of the park tables. As people walked past the line, Bart visited from time to time with former clients, conversations consisting usually of "What have you been up to?", or sometimes, "I really appreciated your help when my son died."

Recognition was hit or miss with past clients. They did not recognize him in shorts and his black "Lithuania" T-shirt. He did not recognize them because, old and grey, they all looked the same. He remembered few of their names and, after a few embarrassments, didn't even try to introduce Higg.

Bart thought of only three things as he inched along in the food line: One, hunger; two, shade; and three, how much longer he had to listen to Higg? Higg did not converse. He lectured and asked no questions of his listener. His smallest unit of "conversation" was the paragraph, more often the page or the chapter. And although he specialized in heating, ventilating and air conditioning; he knew, and would talk about, all fields of construction. Today he talked about parking lots, a subject that held Bart's interest for but a short time. Nevertheless, oblivious to his listener, Higg addressed construction, layering, capacity, usage, legal requirements, and striping—all in detail, all in his unmodulated drone without inflection or pause.

Bart missed large portions of Higg's monologue, and his mind wandered to the rolling green lawn of the park, the kids playing Frisbee, the not-so confidential conversations of the others in line, although from time to time he did smile and nod his head. Higg's long discourse reminded Bart of Benny, a former client, who also talked non-stop. But unlike Higg, Benny could have written comedy. If you asked Benny the time, he'd say something like, "You know, I bought this watch in 19 and 42, and at the time my wife, Bessie, she was pregnant with Tim, I think you've met Tim, and. . . . And off you'd go down memory lane. But after all, you did ask about time. Bart began to laugh remembering Benny until he realized Higg had stopped talking.

Good going Bart. Maybe you can follow up by telling him you're hot for his wife. This was supposed to be a good time for Higg. "I'm sorry Higg. My mind was elsewhere. Your construction expertise reminded me of Benny, a former client who, like you, had extensive knowledge. He could lecture at length on many subjects, especially world history. I think I'm tired today."

Higg said nothing. Just nodded. "I know the feeling. I'm tired most days, tired—and yellow."

As they approached the food service, one of the cooks, a former drinking buddy of Bart's, had sat a dead naked chicken, soon to be cooked and eaten, on the side of the service table with its legs hung over the edge. Fat, pink and goose bumped, it looked like a plump headless baby.

Bart took chicken over tri-tip then asked the server the name of the sitting chicken. His friend said, "Little Bo-Dead". She's peeped her last." Bart asked if all the chickens had a name and were locally sourced. He was told the three chickens on the grill were named Albertson, Safeway and Von, and that they had been bisected with utmost kindness using knives bought from the local Ace Hardware Store." Both laughed. Bart turned to see Higg's reaction, but he had left the line. Saw him talking with Birdie at the picnic table she had been holding for them. Once again, Bart hadn't thought about Higg. Higg, his guest who might die soon. Maybe he should go for the brass ring, suggest a visit to a funeral home after the band concert.

Quickly, though, Higg returned. "I never asked Birdie

whether she wanted chicken or beef."

"And?"

"She wants chicken. Probably the little guy sitting on the table, Bo-Peep or whatever his name was. Imagine he doesn't feel much anymore. Nice when you think about it."

"I suppose," said Bart. "What food do you want?"

Higg just shook his head. "Nothing. I will just eat some of Birdie's."

◆ ◆ ◆

Around 9:00 pm, after the concert ended, the threesome walked home and said their goodbyes. Bart returned to his dog, Lily; Higg and Birdie to their separate rooms. It had been a long day for Higg and he was tired. He moved slowly, sat on the side of his bed. After a moment, he got up and went into Birdie's bedroom. "Did you like the barbeque?", he asked.

"I thought it was fun, what with the band concert and people with their blankets on the grass. Nice of Bart to have invited us." Always up, Birdie bounced and moved as she talked.

"What do you think of Bart; what is his story aside from his fascination with you?"

Feeling like Higg had pulled the cover from a painting, Birdie responded lightly. "Oh, I wouldn't say he's fascinated with me. I think I'm the only one around, aside from you and Granny T. And you and he haven't exactly hit it off." She continued getting ready for bed, walked into her bathroom and picked up her toothbrush. "He doesn't seem to go out much. Think he sees a doctor every so often. Takes piano lessons, but you know that. His kids arranged the lessons, and his son pays for them. Basically, a retired lawyer who lost his wife. That's about all I know."

Higg, took off his square-framed glasses and rubbed his eyes. Putting them back on his head he said, "I think he's full of himself and looks at others as ignorant children, and I think he asks questions without wanting to know the answers. I could say I built a suspension bridge that just collapsed killing twenty people and he would say, 'Oh, my, can't imagine the liability from that' and then he would tell a joke about a dentist who made a fortune selling suspension bridges that didn't kill people. Bart is behind a wall, and he doesn't care what caused the collapse, where it happened, who was killed, who it affected. He flicks you away with the back of his hand. It is all about Bart, all about Bart, and . . ." Higg paused to catch his breath, "and, you know, I am sick of being judged and dismissed. I am a human being, not some animal."

Birdie had never heard Higg speak with such vehemence. Higg dealt in things—material things like buildings, lumber, metal—not people. She felt exposed, frightened. Higg blamed Bart, but she had caused his pain. Big gentle Higg who had done nothing but love her. Had she set him aside for Bart?

She stared at Higg and resisted the urge to cross her arms in front of her. "Come on, Higg, he's not that bad. He's just not an engineer. And he does listen well, at least to me. It's nice to have someone to talk with when I'm down about our kidney situation. But you're right, he does keep his cards close. I imagine practicing law in a small town taught him very early to keep his mouth shut. But who knows? Maybe there's nothing there. More likely, I think he's buried what's there and his jokes just cover things up. I think the loss of Mary probably meant more than he's willing to admit, but I don't know him well enough to ask."

This wasn't true and Birdie knew it. She skated on thin ice and could easily break through. She had been loyal to Higg, cared for him, but it had indeed been a marriage of convenience. He was like a faithful dog, always forgiving, always there when you called him. She fed, brushed him, tried to socialize him. In return he provided for her and adored her. They had no children.

She knew Higg was vulnerable and hurt by her relationship with Bart. But she had found someone to confide in, to share her feelings. She was not about to give it up.

"Birdie, he has no time for me, and that's obvious, and he is off-putting, uncaring, and unfeeling, and everything ends in a joke or some pun."

"How would you have him act?"

"For starters, cut the condescension and smugness, and stop judging me because my interests differ from his. I don't view all lawyers as societal leeches; he should not view all engineers as adults playing with Legos. And, how about 'How are you? How are you doing? Has there been any progress on finding a donor?' or maybe, 'I'm sure it will all turn out well.' We may not share interests, he's obviously not an engineer, but he could give a shit."

Birdie put her arm around his shoulder. "Bart Jones is just a neighbor. I don't have to see him. I'll cancel the piano lessons if it would make you feel better." She kissed his cheek and walked into her bathroom before she said too much. She feared he might follow her.

Ch 26. Empathy

8:00 in the morning. Lily, barking at the sound of the doorbell, races to the front of the house. Bart, still half asleep, throws on pants and his cleanest dirty T-shirt, proceeds quickly to the front door, afraid of what might have happened. Granny T, stands outside, resolute, with a clipboard and handful of political flyers.

Bart relaxes. "Little early to be out and about, Gladys." Bart does not call her Granny T to her face.

Without responding, Granny pushes a red, white and blue hand-out at Bart. She is gathering signatures to propose a new city ordinance which will address "the heinous wrongdoing" of city authorities. As far as Bart can figure out, the ordinance will require the city to offer free carwashes to citizens who park their cars under bird-filled community trees.

Looking at Granny, Bart suspects she dressed in the dark for this important political work. Guesses she kept the light off in her bedroom and adjoining bathroom so as not to wake her husband, John, although Bart knew John, a real milk-toast, wouldn't have made a sound if Granny had turned on a searchlight. In any case, Granny had missed her mouth somewhat with her lipstick and created a good imitation of a Mardi Gras clown. And she had completed her outfit by skipping two buttons on her pink cardigan making one side longer than the other. Somewhat fascinated, Bart watched and listened with remarkable self-control as Granny forcefully argued the merits of mandatory bird-poop cleanup. In the end, Bart signed the petition and escaped in mirth and wonderment of what he had just witnessed.

Later that morning and amused from his meeting with Granny T, Bart recounted the story to Dr. James and told him of a similar occurrence with Hugo, an eccentric client of long ago.

Hugo built low-end motels in high-end tourist destinations and had become rich in the process. Hugo had a dutiful, if simple wife—Bart always thought she had been mail-ordered—and a house full of useless children, the youngest of which was about 30. Hugo never did anything by the book and was in constant need of a lawyer to get him out of his latest mess. Always enthusiastic, Hugo talked in a disjointed staccato manner flitting from one subject to another. He usually would agree with everything Bart suggested and then do exactly what he wanted. But he paid his bills and was never boring.

This particular meeting took place in the office of Hugo's CPA. Hugo, who was years older than his wife, had asked for advice on transferring a particular motel property to his much-younger family. Mid-discussion, Hugo started to squirm and left the room to use the bathroom. Returning minutes later, the meeting resumed, but Hugo wasn't listening. While Bart talked on about legal options, basically advising against what Hugo had in mind, Hugo focused on his hand, first with furtive sniffs, and later with a full nose.

"I just continued talking," Bart remembered, "and experienced a 'Don't you dare look at me moment' with his CPA. Both of us lost it after the meeting. But, Dr. James, both Hugo and Granny T escaped embarrassment."

"Well, yes, Granny T escaped embarrassment until she got to the next house. You ever think of giving her a heads up on the makeup and the sweater so she could avoid later embarrassment?"

"No, I didn't." Bart winked, "She wasn't my client."

"You didn't think about saving her further embarrassment?"

"No. I didn't think about it. Get real. Here's the town gossip in a clown outfit, crusading about bird poop and I'm supposed to think about saving her embarrassment? If anything, she deserved it."

"And Hugo. An elderly man who finds himself in an

embarrassing position?"

"What should I have done? Offered him an antiseptic wipe? Told him to go wash his hands?"

"No, felt badly for him, sympathized with his plight."

"Oh, please. I didn't embarrass him. And people are funny in case you hadn't noticed. Oftentimes, saving people embarrassment, saving yourself embarrassment, is the best you can do. I'll give you an example and you can tell me what I should have done.

"At a legal conference, my wife and I had lunch at a rather elegant hotel dining room, one of those thickly carpeted rooms where one hears only muffled voices and the clink of glassware. On this occasion, a rather large, elegantly dressed lady dined alone. I have no idea why she was alone or large. I still remember the pastel green of her dress.

Anyway, we didn't pay much attention to her until she got up to leave and found herself stuck in the table armchair. When she got up, so did her chair. Quickly an attentive wait-staff, consisting of the maître d' and two others, extracted her. Two held the chair; one pulled her out. There wasn't a sound in the entire restaurant, and all tried to look away. Everyone in that place felt her embarrassment and did their best to minimize it. The scene remains with me to this day, but in hindsight I find it somewhat amusing."

"So in all cases you sought to minimize embarrassment—yours and theirs. And two of them were not your clients. That part is good. And do you think caring and good manners are the same thing? Can you have one without the other? Can you have good manners and not care, or care and not have good manners?"

Before Bart could answer, a large gold-colored car pulled in back of the office and commenced a parking dance that must have taken two full minutes. The next patient had arrived. They were out of time.

"Think about it."

Getting out of his chair, Bart said, "People are funny whether you care or simply have good manners. They do funny things: get stuck in chairs, get pooped on by birds. I'm gonna laugh, maybe just to myself, whether I care or not."

Ch 27. Furniture

Taking in the sun, Higg sat in the white plastic chair outside the music studio. At the edge of the cement patio a small lizard did the same thing. Maybe he was becoming cold blooded like the lizard. These days he felt like one. He was not yellow today, not jaundiced, but white, a speckled brown-white, the color of an unearthed mushroom.

From the patio, he could see oaks, brush, fields of dry grass. He could see chrysanthemums in pots, and houses, and streets, and curbs, and dogs, and people. He wouldn't see them much longer, though he would like to. And, what's more, he could do nothing about it. His kidney failed him. He knew his cancer had returned, but he had no confirmation. When he was gone, Birdie would think of him from time to time. The thought warmed him.

Birdie would be left with Bart and, Higg hoped, be happy. Bart mocked him, treated him as if he were a piece of furniture without substance or feeling. Bart would take Higg's greatest treasure and do so with impunity. He would not think about Higg or the pain he had caused him.

Condescension, banter, always a story, always a joke. Deflect, obfuscate. He focuses on Birdie, plays to Birdie. I don't exist; I'm not in the room. He wants Birdie, and in his mind I don't stand in the way. I am not there.

He pushed himself from the chair. He would talk with Bart, tell him how he felt, what he was losing. He would show Bart the hurt, stab into that smug condescension if he had to. Maybe Bart would feel something.

As he walked the path between the houses. Higg felt lightheaded, as if he had not eaten in many hours. Not a good start to a confrontation, but he liked the idea of collapsing on Bart's floor. Maybe Bart finally would see him as Higg, a neighbor, a human being with feelings. More likely Bart would just step over him and fetch Birdie.

Without knocking, he walked through the unlocked kitchen door where Bart's dog, Lily, greeted him with great ruckus. A disheveled and uncertain Bart soon appeared.

"Is everything OK?"

"No," said Higg, "It is not. We need to talk." Higg, fragile and pale, lunged for a kitchen counter to support himself. Out of breath, he said, "I am not going to be around much longer, and I have some things to say to you before I go and you will not like what I have to say, but out of respect for a dying man, who I know you find boring and inconvenient, I am going to say what I want to say, and you are going to listen." He made eye contact with Bart and did not look away.

Bart carried a chair to Higg, said "Higg, please sit." Bart took a step back. "You . . . want to sit down?"," said Bart? "

"No," Higg said, "I will stand." He would be in charge this morning, say what he wanted to say.

Bart started again to talk, but Higg stopped him with a gesture. Leaning against the kitchen island, he said, "I came to tell you about me, Marvin Higgins, who I am and what I care about. I want to talk to you about respect and feelings and about loss and ending. I know you went through the loss of Mary, but I'm not sure her loss taught you much, except to shield yourself from other people.

"Bart, I am dying and I am losing my precious wife in the process. You do not seem to know that, or maybe you just do not care, but you do know I am not like you: I don't tell funny stories; I am never the life of the party, assuming I am even invited. I have never been able to make people laugh with me; I have always been able to make people laugh at me. I have tried to do right by people, but they take what I give them and expect more, as if my job were to give and theirs to take."

Bart said nothing, fidgeted with his clothing and looked uncomfortable. "Bart, I am dying, and I am losing my precious wife in the process. You do not seem to know that, or maybe you just do not care, but you do know I am not like you, and you've have probably guessed that since I do not tell funny stories. I am never the life of the party, assuming I am even invited.

"I was always the number one student in my classes from grade school through my graduate work in mechanical engineering. People respected my intelligence and my academic success, but behind my back they made fun of me, as if I had no feelings, and did not hear the cruel jokes and see Marvin Higgins imitations.

"My parents did not help: my mother studied and wrote on ancient languages and was lost in herself; my father studied and wrote about philosophy and mathematics, talked of Wittgenstein and Plato, and lived within a world of symbols. I was a lonely kid who, Birdie would say, needed socialization, a concept unknown to both of my parents."

Out of breath, Higg paused his uninflected monologue, looked hard at Bart who sat uncomfortably in his chair.

"In high school and college, I had mind-only dates and loves, because real dates did not turn out well on those rare occasions when someone accepted, and though And though I helped students with their courses, that is as far as it went: they , because they wanted my help; they did not want me. As I got older, I stopped asking, realized my qualities, my personality, were not what people wanted, not, I suppose, what people could tolerate, and I felt cursed, condemned to an unhappy solitary life. Then I got used to a solitary life, but I had hope; every time I looked at a girl I had hope. Out of breath and beginning to sweat, Higg stopped talking. Bart said, "Are you sure you don't want to sit?" Let me get you a chair."

"No," Higg said, "please just listen. I will be done soon, just give me a moment. Bart stared at Higg and moved closer to him, as if to reach out if need be.

ASU," said Higg, "I met Birdie and her roommate, Martha.

They were vibrant, active, both played softball and brought life to anyone near, and I hung out around them, planned my days to intercept them, but they didn't seem to mind. I was smitten by Birdie, her energy, her niceness, and I dreamed of taking care of her, dreamed of loving her and having her love me. I couldn't keep my eyes off her. I had to keep myself from following her around campus, from staring at her. I watched every home softball game. "

"You must have done something right."

"No, it was hopeless, an unrequited fantasy. Birdie treated me with respect and kindness, but she loved only Bite, Bite with his swagger, aviator glasses and money. He was everything I wasn't.

"And then he dumped her—not just dumped her, left school, vanished; and, as I think she told you, left her in trouble." Higg stopped, made a noise as if stifling a sob. Then, in a rough voice, he said, "For awhile, it took away her sparkle. But times." Higg once again paused. The memory still gave him pain. He sighed. With a slight moan, he said, "Times were different then. Birdie was pregnant and unmarried and faced loss of her scholarship and a return in disgrace to a small town in rural Minnesota.

"A week or so later, Birdie's roommate, Martha, came to me, suggested I marry Birdie, said it would not be real, said it would just last until something could be worked out. I thought my dreams had come true. We drove to Las Vegas and married. And we were married, married for a month until she miscarried.

"And then we continued as if nothing had happened. Two students going their separate ways. Whether it was lack of inertia, Birdie's Catholicism, memories of Bite, fear of shame— I don't know, we stayed married, and later when she graduated and had no money, I took her in, and we became roommates. I never touched her; it was purely financial. And, probably like a bad penny, I never moved out and we are together still, and I have loved her, and my joy has been in loving her and sharing her life." Higg began to tear up and could not continue.

Bart took Higg's arm, "Well, you've done something right, you're still together. But you look exhausted. I think we should be getting you back . . . "

"No," Higg said, "I am not done, and I want to talk about you, Bart Jones, and I want you to listen. I am dying, and as my life comes to an end, give up your selfish arrogance and disdain, give up trying to take away the most precious thing I have ever had. Treat me as a person with feelings. Think about me for once, me, my last days, my final memories."

Higg paused, gathered his strength. "I may be the big faithful dog about to be put down, but I deserve to be put down with kindness and dignity, and I know you care for Birdie, and I know she cares for you, but please don't take her until I'm gone." Higg turned and started toward the door.

To Bart the scene played out in slow motion as Higg, with his weakened frame, made his way across the patio. Maybe for the first time Bart saw the whole person.

"I. . . I have focused on Birdie," Bart said. "She's scared about the future."

Higg turned and faced him. "And Higg, Marvin Higgins, have you thought about him?"

Bart said nothing.

"Well in these last few days, how about treating me as a real person—like I exist? How about, 'Hello, how are you, how are you feeling today?' How about listening to me and not blowing me off with one-line jokes? I am dying, Bart. I am losing my life, and I am losing my world in Birdie." He staggered. Bart caught him before he could fall.

"I do not need your help."

"Yes, you do. Let's get you home."

They walked across the field together. When they got to the patio, Higg said, "I just need to sit. Put me in the white chair. I like to feel the life around me."

When Bart returned he sat for a long time in the kitchen, thinking of the pain and the hurt he had caused to a good person. When Bart returned, he sat for a long time in the kitchen thinking of the pain and the hurt he had caused to a good person. From the kitchen he could see the mirror on the far living room wall, see himself, Bart Jones, in unforgiving reflection.

He sat in the kitchen for another ten minutes, finally got up and walked slowly into his office. Dropping into his big office chair, he rested his elbows and laid his head on his desk with his head in. Higg had spoken the truth and both he and Higg knew it. Higg's monotone, his drone, the slow clock-like cadence of his hands. voice made listening to that truth sheer torture. He had never felt so small. groaned. Nevertheless, he had to make amends.

Ch 28. An Offering

3:16 am Bart rolled on his left side, got up and used the john, then returned to bed where Higg, once again, recited Bart's insensitive, unfeeling behavior, and where Bart, once again, watched Higg's near collapse on the kitchen floor.

After 20 minutes, Bart sat up in bed and turned on the light. He tried reading but only turned pages. Donate a kidney or forget the whole thing? He could make amends, maybe save Higg's life and his marriage. He could do right by Higg. He wasn't so sure about Birdie.

He put the book aside and turned off the light. He would donate to Higg and save Higg's life if only for a time. Higg would live, Bart would be the savior.

In the morning light, he wasn't so sure. He hated hospitals with their white walls and sterile smell of antiseptic. He hated "procedures" with knives and doctors. And he knew he would lose Birdie, and he hated that thought most of all. But he had made a decision, and if he were going to do this thing, he needed to talk with Higg.

From the trail Bart could see Higg reading in one of the white plastic chairs outside the piano studio. The sky, dark to the east, looked uncertain as if it might rain, and Bart hoped Higg would stay outside until he got there. A little early for rain, thought Bart, still technically summer, but it would be nice to see things grow again.

He stepped onto the patio.

"Birdie is not here," Higg said in his annoying monotone. "She has gone to the store, and I am not sure when she will be back."

"I didn't come to talk with Birdie. I came to talk with you."

Perhaps thinking of his recent meeting with Bart, Higg put his book down and motioned Bart to a chair.

Bart said, "It may rain soon."

"Yes," said Higg. "We certainly need it. Everything is dead or dying."

After a slight pause, Bart looked Higg in the eye and said, "Higg, I have two healthy kidneys. I can donate one to you if you'll let me."

Higg said nothing, just stared. Bart could feel Higg's mental struggle. He, Bart Jones, the arrogant prick who would destroy Higg's marriage, disparaged him, demeaned him—now offered him life.

"Why would you do that? Do nothing and Birdie is yours. On the other hand, in saving me you get forgiveness, become a hero in the eyes of Birdie, and you put me forever in your debt." He looked off in the distance. ". . . though I may still die."

"I guess," said Bart. "All of the above. I've had my own problems and, as you have pointed out to me, haven't always acted as I should. But people can change, and I'd like to do something worthwhile to make up for my behavior." After a moment Bart once again talked with enthusiasm. "Besides, life is short, and I may need points in order to spend less time in the heat below. So I think we should bury the hatchet and become blood brothers."

Higg did not move; his eyes seemed cold and apathetic, and there was an unusual bitterness in his voice. "Just like that," he said, "we snap our fingers and all is well." Higg sat up in his chair, stiffened. Looking Bart in the eye, he said, "Bart, you have courted my wife, turned my marriage upside down. I will not make you a hero or a savior. And I would rather die than be in your debt." He paused, his hard look unforgiving. "So no. Thank you for your offer, but no."

Bart sat in silence feeling chastised and embarrassed. He had feared this response even though relieved by it. In a strange way, he wondered if he would have made the same decision if roles had been reversed. Would he have been as noble as Higg?

Gazing over the adjacent field, Higg said, "It is tough to turn down life. Does Birdie know about this?"

"No. I haven't talked with her. And Higg, I think you're being unfair to her. Day in, day out she watches you suffer and weaken. She comes next door for half an hour to get away from the sadness, the storm. I'm just someone to talk to. And Higg, your wife is a lady; she has been true to her vows.

The first drops of rain had begun to fall. Higg stood. Bart said, "Higg, she's not in love with me. She may be in love for a brief moment with safety, a warm place out of the darkness, out of danger. And then she returns to you."

Higg walked toward the patio door no longer paying attention to Bart. Bart said, "It's me that needs forgiveness. As you have pointed out, I have not treated you with respect. I hide my feelings behind a blanket of humor. I'm seeing a psychiatrist for that. But you need to live for you and for Birdie, not for me. I hope you'll reconsider."

Higg continued walking, finally turned. "Bart, I don't want to let you save my life. Go home. Leave me . . . leave us alone." He went into the house, closed the door.

Bart stood for a time on the patio looking at the closed door. Then soaked and feeling defeated, he bowed his head and returned home.

Ch 29. Ray

"To a point," said Dr. James, "all benefit from a gift. The recipient, the 'donee' in your legal speak, receives something, feels good, is happy. The giver, the donor, is pleasured by the feelings of another person: their smile, their appreciation. But you have offered Higg life, and he has turned you down, turned you down with bitterness. How does that make you feel?"

"Yesterday I felt ashamed. Today I'm not so sure." Bart crossed his arms, raised his chin toward the doctor.

Dr. James raised a hand toward Bart as if to calm him. "Let's just talk. Tell me what you're thinking about."

Bart said, "I'm thinking about Higg, his feelings . . . thinking, I guess, the way you want me to think. But I don't feel good about things, don't feel good about your advice." Bart stopped talking, waited for a response.

"Go on."

"I don't know. Maybe you're right. Maybe it was a question of timing, of my not seeing Higg the person until it was too late. I do know I can't show my face next door; I'm not happy about that. I think, as I always did, that in sharing feelings you give of yourself, and I know I can give only so much." Bart avoided the eyes of the doctor and took a deep breath. "Maybe I just need a break from these sessions."

After a moment Dr. James said, "Well, you've paid for today and you have 45 minutes left. Why don't we leave Higg and Birdie alone for the present and tell me about your friend, the one you said also had trouble with a kidney transplant."

"I suppose I can do that. Not sure what you'll learn. Like me, my friend Ray got into the mess by himself."

Dr. James nodded.

Bart leaned forward in his chair and took a moment to collect his thoughts. "Many years ago, I worked in the legal department of a large New York investment firm. Upon my arrival in the city, I stood with a friend outside Chase Manhattan Plaza and watched a parking enforcement officer ("meter maid" in those days), ticket cars in front of expired parking meters. Nothing unusual; however, the meter reader did not ticket all of the cars in front of expired meters, but passed by about a third of them. It turned out the "skipped" cars all belonged to a major business located near the plaza. Ray, the firm employee tasked with showing me around, said, "No big deal. They take care of the cops.'

Bart stretched and sat up straight in his chair. "At the time, I doubted this was true, but at lunch that day, Ray regaled me with stories of New York corruption, ranging from putting money in the fold of your driver's license to avoid a ticket at a traffic stop, to giving money, beer, whatever to sanit workers to avoid their flattening your trash cans. My favorite, though, was my commute to work, which reminded me that I wasn't in Kansas anymore.

I worked in an office building on Park Avenue. Each day I rode an elevator to my office on the 39th floor. And each day I looked at the prominently displayed certificate that certified the elevator inspected and safe. And each day, suspended oh-so-many floors above the hard pavement below, I wondered if they'd paid off the inspector. Was this the day I would take a fast trip to the basement? When I raised this question, New Yorkers just shrugged their shoulders. They referred to these types of payments as 'greasing the skids' or 'keeping the machine well oiled.'

Dr. James said, "What does all this, uh. . . graft have to do with a kidney donation?"

"Well I suppose it excuses Ray's behavior in advance, shows the culture in which Ray—I'll talk about Ray in a second —grew up: a culture of commonplace, but required payments to get the service or product you needed, wanted, or were entitled to.

"Now, with that background, I will tell you the story of Ray and the kidney. Ray and I worked together as attorneys in New York. Ray was short with red hair, wore a rather ill-fitting toupee and dressed in suits with squared-off shoulders. He constantly sweated no matter how cold the weather and as a result his face was always wet, his shirt collar open and his tie askew. Ray lived on Decatur Avenue in the South Bronx apartment he'd grown up in, and talked with the rough accent of gangster movies, an accent which masked a high intelligence. Fordham Prep, Fordham, and Fordham Law insured him a place in the sun; nevertheless, his edges needed filing.

"On a vacation to Alaska, of all places, Ray met and fell in love with Deena, and thereafter spent six months and most of his savings flying back and forth to Alaska. Deena, like Higg, needed a kidney to live. Unlike Higg, Deena had no disqualifying medical history, only a distant place on the state registration list, so far down she most likely would die before receiving a transplant. And Ray, with a conflicting blood type, could not be her donor.

"As time passed, Deena became increasingly despondent, struggled to keep up her spirits, begin to see her glass half empty. Ray told her to keep the faith, trust things would work out. And things did work out, although it took Ray several flights to Alaska and some serious borrowed money to 'revise' the list and procure the needed transplant. Ray never went into details. No one is quite sure what transpired, only that Deena received notice a donor kidney had become available. Ray said she was like a little kid on Christmas morning. On January 12, she underwent a successful operation.

"After the operation, according to Ray, Deena lay in her bed with its pastel blue sheets and frilly pillowcases, happily recuperating, talking of her life to come.' He recalled most of his conversation with Deena in detail, remembered her saying,

"I feel so fortunate, so lucky I received a donation. I don't know what happened. One day I'm at the bottom of the list. The next day I'm at the top."

"Ray said he should have kept his mouth shut. Like an idiot, he didn't. Told her Santa had helped with the list.

"He said Deena at first didn't understand what he meant. Then, horrified, realizing what Ray had done, she began to cry. Tears, shaking, sobbing. When she finally stopped, in a quiet voice she said, 'Ray, you've stolen someone's life. You have given me their place and they're now going to die.'

"He remembered saying, 'Deena, any low number takes the place of a high number. If you had drawn number one, you would have taken the place of many with higher numbers. Would they have died because of you?' No, they would have died because they drew a high number.

"Ray said she did not respond. Remembered only looking out the window to make the silence less obtrusive. Deena said, 'I want you to leave. I can't accept what you have done, what I have done. Please just leave.'

"She turned in bed toward the wall and would say nothing further. After several minutes—Ray said it felt like an hour—he laid the flowers he had brought on her bed and left. After that, Deena refused to see or talk with him. He had committed murder and involved her. He said he stayed on for a week or so, then flew back to New York. She would not take his calls nor answer his letters. He never saw Deena again.

"Unfortunately, Ray's trials did not end. In order to finance the operation and the rearrangement of the list, Ray had borrowed money from the mob at 100% interest, payable monthly over five years. No prepayment penalty, but non-payment resulted in pain, or worse. Ray took a second job, then a third. He worked as a tax lawyer during the day, an accountant at nights, and waited tables on weekends. He slept little, often shook from stress and lack of sleep. He lived on practically nothing and became adept at deferring other creditors. Payments were made at the Carol Ruth Inn, a bar in the Bronx.

"On one Saturday Ray could not make his payment because a disgruntled customer, or maybe a competitor, had dynamited the bar leaving nothing but rubble. Ray's lender soon provided him another location at which to make payments.

"Ray survived. It took him two years. He didn't die, although he missed a lot of sleep and got a broken nose once for not making a full payment. I haven't seen Ray since I left New York. I miss him. He was a good friend."

Bart stood and stretched. "That's about it. Ray loved Deena and saved her life, or, in Deena's view, exchanged one life for another."

"Not exactly parallel to your situation," said Dr. James.

"No, though I could argue by making the donation, I'll be exchanging Birdie for Higg. But I won't be bribing public officials. It's my kidney, I'll do whatever I want with it."

"What can you learn from Ray's. . . adventures?"

Bart shrugged, "No good deed goes unpunished?"

The doctor said, "If you think of the person whose place Deena took, arguably not a good deed. The manipulation makes it bad, because Ray replaced chance with intention, put his thumb on the scale if you will, although, as Ray pointed out, anyone with a smaller number takes the place of someone else. After Ray and Deena split, was Ray bitter, philosophical? I'm curious. What do you think?"

"As I've said, Ray had risked much, paid much, and perhaps with Deena, lost much. Deena took his gift and condemned him for taking the life of another. She must have known all along Ray had greased the skids. I think she wanted the kidney, not Ray. But Ray was happy. After everything, Ray felt good about saving Deena's life, even after two rough years where he owed money to the mob and was in danger of having his bribery exposed and losing his law license. And he had lost his love. But, as I said, after everything, Ray was pleased with what he had done. Said it was worth it, or so he told everyone."

"Are you like Ray? Do you offer a kidney to one you love? And, if she stays with Higg, will it be worth it?"

"The one I love? No, I don't love Higg."

"Do you love Mrs. Higgins?"

"I care for her. Not sure I love her." Bart took off his glasses, rubbed his eyes.

"Well, if you didn't offer a kidney for Higg or his wife, who did you offer it for?" The doctor continued without waiting for an answer. "Do you think, after Deena rejected Ray, he felt ashamed for what he had done?"

"No. He was happy for her, thankful for what he had managed to do. He'd saved her life."

"If you were my friend and I was lying hurt, and you offered to help me and I turned you down, would you be ashamed?

"No, confused. . . frustrated maybe."

"Why not ashamed?"

Outside a white SUV pulled up. James checked his watch and brushed off his T-shirt. "I'm afraid our time is almost up, but I'd like to know why you were ashamed when Higg turned you down. You tried to help and he refused. Where's the shame?"

"I didn't. . . I didn't make this offer for Higg, and Higg knew it, knew it had nothing to do with him. I wanted to be the good guy, do the right thing. Yes, I wanted to make up for the way I had treated Higg, but only after Higg called me out. Ray loved Deena. He did what he did for Deena. I never loved Higg; I made this offer for myself."

"Or maybe for Birdie?" The doctor didn't wait for an answer. "So how do you feel about all this?"

"I think I'm back to 'ashamed' since transferring this mess to you didn't work. Higg knew what I'd done to him, to his marriage. He knew this was a feel-good gift for me, and he wasn't about to let Bart Jones be the good guy—even at the cost of his own life. He showed me for what I was." Bart looked down then stared at the window, his mind full of questions. If he had offered his kidney purely out of concern for Higg, would feeling good about what he had done somehow lessen the gift? Giving a kidney, after all, saves someone's life. Can someone give a kidney without feeling satisfaction? And where did Higg fit into this? In rejecting the gift, didn't Higg reject Birdie who had fought so long and hard for his life? If nothing else, should he not accept the gift for her?

"Thoughts," said Dr. James?

"Yeah, many," said Bart. "Interesting questions without answers. Too many to discuss when we're out of time." He looked straight at the doctor. "I'm sorry about what I said to you. Well, not that sorry, that's why you get the big bucks. No, I apologize. I was wrong. These sessions, you, have helped me understand things, understand myself. In any case, I'm now free. Higg either lives or dies. Whatever my motives, I did make the offer to save him. If he dies, maybe there's a future for Birdie and me. If he lives, well, I'll just take it one step at a time, see if I can make amends."

On his arrival home, Lily greeted Bart with tail wags and dog kisses. Somebody loved him even though at the moment he didn't love himself. He realized he had caused his defeat and humiliation by loving only himself. Higg saw Bart for what he was, and given the choice between death and ennobling Bart, had chosen death. A next step for Bart? A way out? His head was so filled with emotion, he could not think. He hugged Lily and decided to take her for a walk.

Ch 30. Reflections

Friday night, the week over, time to play, party, kick back. Time to rest after a long week. And despite teaching piano only two days a week, Birdie looked forward to Friday night. Friday night was still special—until it came.

Birdie noticed the emptiness first. With Higg's condition, they had stopped entertaining and seldom went out. She still anticipated Friday night. She waited all week, and then it was as if she went to sleep on Christmas Eve with a tree full of presents and woke with gifts put away and the family gone.

Birdie sat this Friday evening at the kitchen table watching the day fade into darkness. Aside from an occasional car, there was no sound outside. The smells of chicken and broccoli still lingered. Otherwise, all had been cleaned and put away. Her several house plants, placed inconveniently on the tops of cupboards, sagged with dryness. They needed water. Tomorrow. She would do that tomorrow.

Birdie was not tired. Weary perhaps, but not tired. Her head rested on her arms; her eyes were closed. She didn't want to move, wanted only to keep herself from thinking. Free her mind from troublesome thoughts. Tabula rasa, a good goal.

She could not do it. Asleep in his chair, Higg's body slowly failed him. Kind, gentle Higg. He had rescued her, done nothing but give. She knew he loved her, had known it from the day of college registration. He could not keep his eyes off her then or now.

She had well repaid him; looked after him, coached him, thanked him. She had stayed with him. But they were never lovers. No roses. No moonlight. Only a saving marriage she often thought of as a still life.

Bite, her big Texan with his silver buckle and aviator glasses, had captured her, then discarded her pregnant and alone. Yet she often thought of him, felt his strong but gentle touch, his arms around her. Their moments together, secret encounters, explorations, hopes—were part of her. She could remember his smell, his cockiness; she could see his unbuttoned white shirt and crooked smile.

But Bite had gone, and Birdie had been loyal. She had done everything in her power to find a donor for Higg, to save his life: hours with kidney banks, talks with potential donors, requests placed on social media. Nothing. She could not defeat his age and cancer. Yes, in unguarded moments she dreamed of romance, a new life where she could love as well as be loved.

Outside, a cold restless wind moved fog around, and as it weaved and flowed, hid then revealed the trees and flowers of another world. Birdie felt the cold of the house. The furnace, which usually came on at this hour, had been turned off for the summer and not yet revived. Higg slept, head askew in his overstuffed chair. She covered him with a small blanket, then having no other demands on her, sat quietly.

She supposed all couples, all people who have lived together for years, end their lives waiting, with one partner floating downstream and the other tied to the pier. Birdie could untie and recover Higg, or she could let him go, cast off and make her own way upriver. Higg's oncologist thought Higg "cancer free," but Higg had been cancer free before only to have cancer wink at him. His kidney doctor said Higg must replace his diseased and failing kidney, his only kidney, if he were to live. And unlike the doctor, or maybe like him, Birdie believed "diseased" and "failing" meant cancer.

Higg awoke, looked up at Birdie, and waved to her with open hand like a little kid. "How about some light," she said. She switched on the table lamp which flashed and returned to shadow. Higg rubbed his eyes, discarded the blanket and sat up. Birdie, sat on the couch next to his chair, said "How are you feeling?"

"Fine," said Higg. "I waited to talk with you but fell asleep.

"

Birdie picked up the discarded blanket and began to fold it.

"Bart came over today."

"And what did Bart want?"

"He wanted to give me one of his kidneys."

The blanket slipped out of her hands and dropped unfolded to the carpet. "Oh" was all she said, and then, as if talking to a stranger, said "Higg, that's wonderful. After all this time." She kissed the top of his head. "I had almost given up." She turned and walked several steps toward the kitchen, let out a deep breath, then faced her husband with tears in her eyes. This was not about her. Higg had found hope, and that was what mattered. "We should celebrate," she said. She refolded Higg's blanket, fussed with the house plants on the mantel. One of them, she noticed, had died.

Higg watched her, watched her movements, held his hands in his lap. Then, as if he could read her mind, he said "Birdie . . .I turned him down. Nothing has changed."

She took a step back. "I don't understand."

"I turned him down. Accepting a transplant from Bart, from anyone, is not honest and is not fair. I'm in poor health, and I may not survive the operation assuming we can find someone willing to do it, and even if it succeeds, with my cancer I may survive only a short time. It would be a waste. If Bart wants to give a kidney to make himself feel good, he should give it to someone who has life in front of them."

"That's not the way things work," she said. "You never can find the most deserving person. It would be an impossible task and how would you judge?" You give to people you know."

"I love you, Birdie. I know this is hard for you, but I'd like to die with some dignity."

She bit her lip. "Higg, don't do this. Now's not the time

to give up on yourself or us. You don't quit the race at the finish line. I'll drag you across if I have to."

"I'm sorry," he said.

◆ ◆ ◆

Across the field, Bart sat in his office sipping a 110 proof bourbon he had bought in Chattanooga several years before. Industrial grade, its alcohol content masked its taste but numbed his feeling. He had made the offer to Higg; Higg had turned him down. Now he was back to square one, and all he wanted to do was leave it all behind. He imagined a cruise, a long cruise—a month maybe, with lots of ports. He would meet someone.

He saw himself in "open seating," sitting at a lunch table for six. Five women and Bart. All but one polite and welcoming. One was not. Arrogant and condescending, she took offense at almost everything Bart said, which wasn't much. He kept a low profile, knew the rest of the table was behind him. Nevertheless, with her he felt like a garbage worker who had crashed a white tie affair.

"I don't see how you can live in California," Ms. Arrogant said with her Boston accent. "By the time you get up in the morning, everything has already happened."

This comment so stunned Bart that at first he could only stare at her. Finally, he said, "It's OK. I live in London half the year. And," he said with a wink and a smile, "the people in California are nice." Bart could tell most of the table were widows and eager to meet him, and, truth be told, he them. Ms. Arrogant obviously had issues.

Bart saw himself leaving the table, wishing the group a pleasant afternoon and wandering out on deck to watch the ocean race by. But looking out at the passing ocean, he saw

Birdie, knew he should have stayed to help her. Higg's death would be difficult even though expected. Maybe they'd mix his ashes with cement, use him for paving stones. "The Martin Higgins Memorial Pathway dedicated to those who have made concrete their life's work." An awful thought, Bart. Higg was a decent person, honorable, who had done right by Birdie. And, better still, he no longer was Bart's problem. Higg had released him, set him free.

This afternoon Bart would go to a whiskey tasting and then take a nap until 5:00 when the classical violin/piano duet played in the Sapphire Lounge. And, depending on the number of gin and tonics he drank during the performance, either order room service or float into dinner. He might meet someone in the classical lounge, or maybe he'd wonder down to the blues venue and dance. Most probably he would opt for the dining room and its imaginative menu.

At dinner he would recognize one of the people from lunch. She would greet Bart with a smile and apologize for Arrogant's behavior. "I don't know who she was. Hadn't seen her before lunch today. I think all of us at that table were embarrassed."

They would talk the rest of the evening. She called herself "Katy", short for Katerina. She lived in Morgantown, West Virginia, home of the WVU Medical School, where she had taught in the Psychiatry Department. Now a professor emeritus, she had specialized in abnormal psychology.

Bart said, "Is there a definition of "normal" from which one can determine when someone is abnormal?" Bart thought about Big Brother, East Germany and the USSR.

"No," she said, "we're not talking about political or social norms, we're talking psychosis—about people who think they're Jesus or are being followed by the ghost of Genghis Kahn and commanded to kill cats."

"Kill cats, eh?" Bart told of Mary's beloved cat who

could ransack any unlocked cupboard or closet and create a snowstorm from any available roll of toilet paper. He said he would have sacrificed the cat to Genghis, but it had run off. Bart would see Katy the rest of the cruise. Both delighted in each other's presence. Bart wondered what it would be like to live in Morgantown.

But he was not on a ship. And Katy, if she existed, 3000 miles away. Birdie and Higg were right next door, across a short field. He could go away now, but they would go with him. He sat at his desk staring out at a sea of fog. He would not go on a cruise. He would stay here for Birdie. Besides Morgantown was too close to Boston and Ms. Arrogant.

Ch 31. Redux

Higg had refused Bart's offer of a healthy kidney, a kidney that could continue Higg's life, at least for a time—maybe a long time, maybe not. Birdie could change his mind, convince him to accept and live awhile longer. Lots of things she could do if she wanted.

Higg now breathed without sound and Birdie realized he stood looking at her. "I think you're unhappy with me," he said.

"Come, sit by me," she said. He sat, and she took his hand in both of hers. She did not look at him. "I'm hurt, Higg. I think you doubt me. Bart has indeed been good to me, helped me in my struggle to save you. I've spent the last year searching, searching for someone who would donate a kidney to an older man with a history of cancer. Bart has stood by me, and he has now offered you life. And you turn him down.

"I understand your feelings. He has treated you like you don't exist. You think he covets your wife and has damaged your marriage." She looked up at him and squeezed his hand. "You believe, probably know, that Bart makes this gift for Bart, not for you. And you know people will praise him, and he will feel righteous and good for what he has done. And you also know, for the rest of your life, you will be in his debt; in debt to the man who has hurt you most.

"But he hasn't stolen your love or ruined your marriage. I'm still here, and if I had wanted Bart Jones, I had only to do nothing and wait. Honey, we failed to find a donor after more than a year of trying, and we have no other prospects. None.

"It's true. Bart is a good friend and has been very kind to me. But you're my husband. And if you don't accept this kidney donation, you die. So live and keep the girl."

"You want me to live?"

She almost hit him. "Oh, my God, Higg. After all we've been through. Do you think you're the only one here?"

He held up his hands. "I am sorry. I have not been fair to you."

Birdie went into the kitchen, poured herself a glass of red wine. I've not been fair to myself. She stood at the counter, looked around the kitchen, remembered the times she had spent cooking for Higg, trying to bring cheer into his life. Thought of Bart and pies and talks and smiles. It wasn't to be. She reached for the glass of wine and knocked it over. A large puddle of red expanded on cold granite. She looked at the broken glass and began to cry.

Higg waited until 10 o'clock the following morning to seek Bart. The fog had lifted and the sun, yellow and white, backlit and darkened the trees. Bart sat at his desk with his fourth cup of coffee trying to decide if he wanted to read the Wall Street Journal or continue with *Portrait of a Lady*. Bart read novels when he didn't like the news, and since retirement he had become well read. Probably a sign of aging or turning into his parents. Today, though, he wasn't liking Isabel Archer's decisions and couldn't tolerate national events. So he focused on the field outside his office window, sipped his coffee, and saluted the small oak, which still waived its green flags after the bone-dry summer. Most of its friends had died.

Bart felt relieved this morning and free. Dr. James had been right. Bart had made the offer for himself, to be the good guy. Stupid decision really, and it scared him after making it. But with the sunshine and Higg's refusal, he had that lean-back-and-put-up-your-feet feeling.

Chimes at the door terminated his reverie. Walking to the front of the house, Bart saw Higg standing in shadow on his porch. Sallow complexion, rumpled grey slacks. His thick-framed black glasses right out of Engineering Quarterly. Higg fidgeted, stared at his feet. He had changed his mind. No good deed goes unpunished, thought Bart.

Regretting his fourth cup of coffee, Bart hid in the darkness of his living room until he feared Higg would ring again. He had lost but would make the best of it. Time to be Bart.

"Don't tell me," said Bart. "You want my penis as well as my kidney."

"Actually," said Higg in a rare moment of humor, "I came solely for your balls, but I'll settle for a kidney, if the offer still is open."

Bart said nothing, his day ruined. Higg should at least twist in the wind, if only for a moment. "Yes, it's still open. I knew you would change your mind, so I haven't peed since I made the offer. Wanted the kidney to be nice and fresh." Higg, looking like he might cry, said thank you, mumbled something about not being himself.

In the distance Bart could see a police car. It slowed to a stop at the end of the street. Bart waited. Wanted it to go away. Higg looked around as if to flee, finally said thank you and walked hurriedly across the field to his house.

They would meet later, perhaps over lunch or dinner, to discuss arrangements. Higg would cheat death, at least for a while. Bart, hands in his pockets, walked back across the darkened living room, wondering why he had offered to donate. Feel good or no, he was the loser in this transaction. Get cut open, lose an organ so Higg can ride off into the sunset with Birdie.

The right thing? Right thing for whom? He could say his doctor refused to perform the procedure, but that wasn't true. And they would know. His urologist and Higg's urologist were in the same group. Even if Higg and Birdie would never know, he would. Stupid. Stupid, stupid, stupid.

Ch 32. Amy

This morning, as a surprise, Sophie had prepared an egg soufflé for her husband, Tom, who usually prepared breakfast for the family. In her confusion she had not wiped her pan thoroughly before starting, and her soufflé ended up looking like a tortilla. Tom had been gracious. Butter cures most things. Except Dad. If only butter worked with Dad.

Wanting help with Dad, Sophie decided to call her brother. She hesitated to make the call; knew she would get little comfort. Some perspective perhaps—maybe like "Your cat is just one of the 50,000 killed annually." Calling her brother was always an experience, more like an approach-avoidance conflict. Sophie wanted his support but knew in advance he would, in his annoyingly confident manner, minimize her concerns. Nate was indifferent to a situation if he could do nothing about it. Thus, when fire threatened his mountain cabin, Nate just shrugged his shoulders and noted Cal Fire had closed the area to all but safety personnel. Said he would address the situation once the area reopened. Either he would have a cabin or an insurance claim. In the meantime, he paid scant attention. She had asked, "Don't you want to know? Aren't you concerned?" And Nate, looking at her as if she were foolish, said "Sure I'm concerned, but there's nothing I can do about it. What would you have me do?"

Nate was Sophie's big brother: her best friend growing up and her worst enemy. He could be the nicest person on earth or just plain spiteful. However, when she really needed someone, when it mattered, he was there. But he had always been a jerk.

She called Nate today on her land line so both could talk at once. Cell phones made that difficult. As usual, Nate's receptionist, Marge answered the call on the second ring. Marge said she would see if "Mr. Jones" was available, even though she had known Sophie for years. Returning to the phone, Marge said "Mr. Jones will be with you shortly." What's up with her?

Sophie wondered. Bad morning? Mr. Jones being his usual self? With luck when Mr. Jones returned "shortly" he would be 3'2" tall. Wishful thinking, and perhaps unlikely. Finally, His Royal Highness came on the line.

"Sophie, my beloved sister, are you pregnant again?"

He's such an ass. "Yes, but this time with an ostrich. I'm looking forward to birthing a gigantic egg. If it comes in time for Easter, I'll let you color it—maybe pink and blue since we won't know the gender until it hatches. And," she said, "you're the logical one to sit on it since you're the biggest . . . ."

"Maybe you should consider a hummer next time. Smaller egg; bigger pecker."

"Actually Nate, an ostrich has a larger beak. Besides hummers have no necks."

"So you called me to discuss birds?"

"No, I called you about our father. My sources tell me he has committed to donate a kidney to Higg, that neighbor he can't stand. His doctors have approved, but I think they forget about his helicopter crash and motorcycle accidents. I don't want him to go ahead, but I can't move him. When I talk to him, he just tells me everything will be alright. I hoped you could do something."

"Transplant's probably not for Higg. As I recall, Dad has the hots for Higg's wife. He's probably getting something on the side."

"Yuck, not a great visual. Our parents having sex gives me the creeps."

"You think people over 60 shouldn't, what, grouse in the goody?"

"I don't know about people over 60, but I never could imagine our parents 'doing it'. The image turns my stomach." Still, she almost giggled.

Sophie could feel his eyes roll.

"Well, now that we've both been immaculately conceived, how can I help you?"

"Well for starters you can be concerned. Our father very well may not survive the procedure."

"OK . . . I'm concerned, and . . . ?"

She fought to control her voice. "Nate, this transplant could kill him. You know his condition after all his accidents. And what's more, Higg, his beloved recipient, has a history of cancer, so this stupid transplant may kill Dad and not save Higg."

"What makes you think he's doing the wrong thing? It seems to me you're thinking about yourself and not about Dad. Saving a life isn't such a bad thing, well, unless the person you save is a jerk. As I recall you were in NICU after you were born."

"Yeah, but nobody gave their life to save mine. Nate, please do something. Reason with him; try to talk him out of it."

"I take it you have failed."

Angry, she stopped talking. Sat down in a kitchen chair and looked through the door at a pile of laundry. Sometimes she thought everything wrong with her was the result of her brother.

"Sophie, I've got to run. I will talk with him. And I apologize for giving you a bad time. I do share your concern. But you have a hundred times more influence with Dad than I do. I have never been Daddy's darling little girl. Dad will thank me for my concern and tell me he's going to do it anyway. But I'll call, visit him, whatever I can do."

In the meantime, good luck with your egg. And watch yourself around heat. You may end up with a hard-boiled child."

Yeah, like my brother.

Feeling clever, Nate scrolled through the research on Amy Rice, now known as Amy Echlin. As a widely published professor of classics, she had not been difficult to find. Living in Larkspur, north of San Francisco, she was within driving distance of his Palo Alto office. At least from her profile, she appeared alone and unattached.

Amy Rice. Married name: Amy Echlin. Age, 67. Professor Emeritus in Classics, University of Indiana. Husband, Albert Echlin (deceased). No children. Author of seven books on the classical Greek period and many professional articles. Winner of multiple prizes and awards including. . .

Somewhat heavy for Dad. But maybe she can light a fire under him or at least show him Mrs. Higgins isn't the sole source of heat.

Nate had not called his dad about the pending transplant. From experience he knew such a call would end badly. Though he had only been a captain, Bart would assume his Marine Commanding General persona with Nate. "I've made the decision, Nate. It's no longer open to question."

Nate was but a solder in the ranks. Nevertheless, he was a solder and a son, and knew much. Dad had regaled him with stories of wine, women and guns, of past escapades, and, once in a rare moment, of Amy, his college love, the one who got away. Dad didn't talk about Amy and hadn't seen her since she left school. Questions about Amy elicited his usual humor defense. "She's probably a circus performer now."

Dad had lived with Amy for two years while both were students at Stanford. According to Dad, theirs was an intense, physical romance, one that had wounded Dad when Amy left. If Nate could put Amy back into Dad's life, maybe Dad might change his mind about a transplant.

So Nate called Amy. Told her of Bart's life, his family, his military and legal career. Told her Bart had lost his wife several years earlier and was now alone. Told her Bart often talked about her—a lie, but she needn't know. Amy, also alone, or maybe just interested, agreed to meet Nate for lunch in Mill Valley.

They met at "Clarissa's Café and Flowers", formerly Throckmorton Coffee, a long-time café located on Throckmorton Avenue, the main street of Mill Valley. Nate had arrived early as was his custom and seated himself where he could watch the door. Online photos of Amy showed a slender, intelligent looking person, but photos lie.

At 12:30, a tall woman, athletic, mid-60s walked into the café. She looked Nate in the eye, came to his table, sat down, threw her hat on the empty chair next to her. "I hope you're Nate. But if you're not, I'd like to meet you."

Wow thought Nate, wishing momentarily he was Bart. "And I, you. You must be Amy."

She smiled. "Yes, I'm Amy, your father's former. . . uh friend. What's on your mind?"

Nate wasn't sure he was up to this, was amazed at the strength and assurance of this woman. He punted. "How 'bout we get something to eat first, you know, eat first talk later."

"That's Italian. My field's Greek. But I suppose you know that. Like you, I did some research."

Feeling translucent, Nate said, "Well then let's talk. But I'd still like to order, if you're game. The menu combines grazing with ordinary, but you should be able to find something. I'll pay."

She looked at him, just looked at him, sighed, relaxed. "You remind me of Bart. As you know, I lost my husband and I, too, am alone. I'd like to see Bart again, if only to reminisce. I've thought of him often. But Bart and Amy were 40-some years ago. And I'm pretty happy where I am.

A waitress appeared bearing blue cloth menus. She spoke with a British accent. "Hello. My name is Margo, and I shall attend you. All our food is fresh and locally sourced. If you have any questions, please ask. I'll give you a few minutes."

"Thank you," said Nate. He looked down at the cloth menu. "Maybe I shouldn't have offered to pay."

"Well, you can watch me eat if you like. Save you some money." She paused. "Changing the subject, why am I talking to you instead of Bart?"

"Well, for starters, Bart doesn't know you're here. You're still the one that got away. Fled to the mysterious East."

"Is Bart OK?"

"He thinks so."

"But. . . "

"Dad has decided to donate a kidney to his neighbor's husband. I'm not sure why. He has no use for the husband. The wife has looked after him a bit since my mom died two years ago. He is grateful to her. There could be more to it than that, I don't know. And I don't know his reasons for this donation. I'm not sure he does."

"So what's the problem? People donate kidneys every day."

"Yes, they do. And Dad's still athletic. . . fit. Un canon as the French would say. But he was in a burning helicopter in Marine training and since then has crashed two motorcycles. His GP and urologist have both OK'd the procedure, but my sister and I are not so optimistic. We fear he may not recover from the operation.' In fact, Sophie told him, 'Why don't you donate both kidneys. You'll probably get the same result.'"

"So. . . you're wanting me to talk Bart out of this transplant?"

"Well, yeah. . . . Wanting you to appear. You are the lost love; the one that got away. I think your reappearance may force him to reexamine his decision. Reconsider what he is doing and why he's doing it."

"I take it you have failed?"

"Fallen absolutely flat."

"Hmm. . . A lot to think about. We should have ordered a bottle of wine."

The lunch at Clarissa's Café and Flowers continued. Wine was ordered and drunk. A good GSM blend compromising conflicting desires for a thin Pinot and a heavy Syrah.

"I loved my two years with Bart. I also realized Amy, Amy the person, was fading. I wanted a career, recognition. I wanted to contribute more to society than pop out little dirty faced bodies. I wanted to be Amy Rice, not Mrs. Bart Jones, nor Mrs. anything else for that matter. So I left. Not because I didn't care for Bart, but because I cared for Amy. It was a different time, a time when most women were subsumed in marriage where they cooked, reared children, and looked out for #1: their husband. Later, as you know, I married. But times had changed. We married as equals.

"My husband has died, and you could say I'm alone. But I sit on a healthy retirement, have friends, recognition, money for travel. Why would I want Bart back in my life? You know, I've packaged those two years. Tied them up with a pretty bow and put them away. I do think of them occasionally, but I don't think I want that box reopened."

"I'm not talking about you. And I don't seek to rekindle your past. I'm talking about saving Bart's life." Nate put down his glass. "Is saving a life important to you? Or do you just deal in dead Greeks?"

Amy grimaced. ". . . Well, from what you've told me, it doesn't seem important to Bart. You tell him if he goes ahead with this transplant he may die. So what does he do? He goes ahead. I don't mind helping people, and yes, I do want him to live. But I can't help dumb."

"Can't or won't. Either way it's the same result." Nate asked for the check. "I appreciate your meeting me here. I can see why Bart was smitten. You're certainly a remarkable person. Is it OK to tell Bart I ran into you, or should we pretend this meeting never happened?"

Amy stared at Nate. Picked up her purse. Looked out the window at the passing cars. "No. Tell him. . . Tell him I'll come and see him."

The following morning, 250 miles to the south, Bart sat in his large, overstuffed chair doing nothing much, trying to wake up. From time to time he drank from a large mug of hot black coffee. He had to leave the house in an hour or so for his piano lesson, but his piano lesson was next door, so he wasn't worried. He should be warming up and practicing, but he didn't feel like it. He now paid for the lessons instead of Nate. He could be as unprepared as he wanted, assuming his teacher would tolerate it, and he knew she would. Mrs. Higgins was his teacher. For the present, Bart was content just to sit, drink, look around. He did notice a hairline crack in the plaster above the front window. Hadn't seen it before. Probably should fix it rather than paint over it.

His mind wandered to a prior therapy session. He had laughed at Granny T with her misapplied makeup and bird-poop petition. Dr. James said Bart should have tried to understand Granny and share her feelings. Bart thought James' viewpoint unrealistic.

Bart did feel somewhat sorry for Granny T and regretted not saving her future embarrassment. She was a sad old lady, just wanting to play a part, have a role. And like most old people, she had become invisible. Bart himself had gone from "Who's Who?" to "Who Are You?", but he doubted Granny ever had been in the first category.

Bart knew little of Granny's past. He did know she had no children and a door mat for a husband. He would guess she had few friends. She might have benefitted from grandchildren although he wasn't sure. But she had no grandchildren. She was nosey and judgmental, stuck a finger into every tender spot she could find. Anything to call attention to herself. Bart understood her behavior. . . or thought he did. But he didn't share her feelings, nor did he want to.

Nate called at 10:00 am and asked about Casa Jones availability. Wasn't certain of the date. Couple of weeks from now. Said he would be with a "friend." What this time, thought Bart? Love interest number 42 or another Northwestern theatre arts Ph.D. focused on changing someone's mind for a client. The former were fungible and, in Bart's opinion, usually deserved better than Nate with his total concentration on work. Nate's tools—actresses, mathematicians, policy wonks—were much more interesting than his ephemeral affairs. Bart loved the dissonance of a person with a 160 IQ playing the vapid tart, chewing Juicy Fruit and wearing a miniskirt. Who was Nate going after this time?

Ch 33. Thoughts of a Summer Night

As she walked across the field, Birdie could see a couple of stars, probably planets she thought. On summer evenings, the rest of the sky hid behind the fog. She felt good. She always did after visiting Bart. She liked his welcoming, Lily's wagging tail, the light in Bart's eyes when she gave him an apple pie or some fresh baked cookies. She liked his weakness for cinnamon and crunchy sugar and his wry sense of humor. In short, time began to run instead of walk when they were together—at least for her. If Higg were gone, would Bart still light up when he saw her? Could he get past Mary?

Mary, of course, lived in memory. And memory files off the edges. Bart would remember his svelte wife, her piercing dark eyes, and her tastefully dressed runner's body. He would remember her smile, her rose scent, her remarkable intelligence, her gift of organization. He would remember her parenting and how she cared for him. He would, she knew, remember the perfect wife.

She could still see Mary dressed in her tennis "whites", a small skinny serious woman who had a knack for getting things done. She had been a good neighbor, Birdie thought, but given to moods. It seemed like some days she just woke mad and biting. She would sully everything and everyone around her, sit on her blue silk couch and tell you her life was a grey wasteland of boredom and emptiness. Even when happy she could be hard to take, with her overwhelming desire for control and order. You could not be laid back around her. A take-charge person, she would seize the floor and not let it go, talk in paragraphs instead of sentences.

Birdie stumbled slightly on a root. Her shoes were wet, and she couldn't remember walking the first part of the trail. She stopped for a moment, breathing in the smells of the wet hay and the neighborhood sycamore trees. Her house lay ahead, submerged in the darkness.

She knew she was a better cook. Mary could read recipes and order from a menu with the best of them. But cooking wasn't her thing, not something she wanted to do. When she did cook, she cooked only healthy foods (her daughter, Sophie, described these as "rabbit foods") creating in her family an unrequited passion for red meat, butter and salt.

Physically, she couldn't imagine replacing Mary. Before she got sick, Mary was 5'2", 120 pounds and usually won her division in any race she entered. Birdie at 5'11", hit the scales at 175. She did have a pretty face, but the rest of her still caught softball for ASU. Bart would be trading a sports car for a truck. But then again, the Ford 150 outsells all the sportscars, at least in America.

She opened the door to the familiar smells of her darkened kitchen. There was no light under Higg's door, or Higg for that matter. She prayed he could not read her mind.

Ch 34. A New Beginning

Following Mary's celebration of life, Sophie, at her father's urging, had taken her mother's ruby ring and some cashmere sweaters. Aside from these items though, Mary's immense closet remained intact, a shrine to Mary, her presence, and the faint rose of her scent. But three years had passed, and Mary would not be back. So one hot Thursday morning, Bart steeled himself and called Fashion Faire, the local thrift center. Kelsie Dahlia, a long-time friend of Mary's, answered the phone. "Kelsie," he said, "I've got about an acre of Mary's clothing, and I can't wear any of it—at least not in public. I'd like to donate it. I should have called you long ago, for some reason I couldn't. . ."

Kelsie said, "Why don't I come over and help you. It'll be easier with two of us. And we must separate clothing anyway in order to sell it."

They met that afternoon. Kelsie, a widow in her 60s, had dark eyes and a pyramid of chocolate brown hair with some white highlights. Full-bodied and short, she reminded Bart of an Italian actress. Kelsie arrived wearing shorts and a low-cut tank top. "I apologize for the outfit, but it can get way too hot in a closet."

Bart nodded. It can get way too hot other places as well, he thought.

They sorted and talked in the large walk-in closet, amidst piles of clothing which they then transferred into giant black trash bags. The closet had small upper widows to let in light, but the windows did not open, and Bart's house, like most houses in the cool coastal climate, was not air conditioned.

After a while, both Bart and Kelsie began to sweat in the heat. Kelsie's tank top clung to her and she leaned and moved as if he weren't there. He felt like a driver passing a freeway accident, knowing he should keep his eyes on the road but captured by the scene. Would Mary have been offended, or amused? He picked up a red nightgown he had given Mary one

Valentine's Day, more gossamer bikini than nightgown. Kelsie said, "Don't tempt me. That would be a whole lot cooler than what I'm wearing."

Bart felt his body respond, then looked away. "Mary wore it only once and found it so embarrassing she never wore it again. She was comfortable with her naked body. Naked was OK, but sex object wasn't. She wore it once and I never saw it again. Sorry, that was a private story. I shouldn't have said anything."

"I think she'd forgive you; I feel the same way. I like to get naked, but not to be embarrassed." She looked Bart in the eye.

"I'm going to get us some water," said Bart and left the closet. He wanted her, his body wanted her, but his head knew an affair with Kelsie would further mess up his life. He stood for a minute or so in front of the open refrigerator, then grabbed two bottles of ice water. Returning to the closet, Bart hoped the moment had passed.

Kelsie said, "I've kept in contact with Sophie. I've always enjoyed her. She was a funny child, often too bright for her own good. Certainly played games with Mrs. Tharp. Anyway, Sophie tells me you're thinking of donating a kidney to Higg."

Frowning, Bart said, "Well 'funny child,' it seems, has been telling stories out of school. But yes, I've pretty much decided to donate. Sophie, as you may know, does not like the idea. She's convinced I will not survive or, best case, will turn myself into a vegetable—probably an eggplant, immobile and purple."

Kelsie leaned over and tossed several black bras into the underwear pile. "She says you and Mrs. Higgins, have become close, thinks Mrs. Higgins may have orchestrated this donation."

"She imagines too much. Mrs. Higgins helped during Mary's last year, and after Mary died, has looked in on me from time to time. She's been stressed lately because of Higg's illness. So, yes, I'd say we've become close, but nothing beyond that. She often brings over food—her apple pies are quite good—and makes sure I'm not dead. We talk most often about Higg. I'd like to think I've helped her with Higg and with the stress she's been under. I don't do much more than listen."

Kelsie said, "I've known the Higgins for a long time. Aside from teaching piano, she volunteers at Fashion Faire and at the Blood Bank. She's a lady in constant motion, active, gets things done. It makes me tired to watch her. "

"I might do the same thing if I were married to Higg," said Bart.

"He is different. But who knows what makes people happy? There must be something there. They've been married for a long time. That's why your kidney donation scares me. As a wife who lost her husband, I would have done almost anything to save his life." She put her hand on Bart's shoulder. "And Bart, I think she will as well. She's married to Higg, and she needs a kidney to save Higg's life. You've got what she wants. Once she gets it, . . ."

A large black spider cut off their conversation. Bart fetched an empty water glass, trapped the spider and carried it outside. He did not kill spiders if he could avoid it, although he made an exception for black widows.

Bart said, "Donating was my idea not hers. She didn't even know about my decision until after I talked with Higg."

"Well, I knew about it." She unfurled a gold scarf from underneath a pile of pant suits. "Bart, I don't know how close you are with Mrs. Higgins. But I like you and don't want you to get hurt. Right now you're a 68-year-old man with a life-saving kidney. Once it's gone, you may be only a 68-year-old man. Here, help me with this bag." But before Bart could help, the bag split showing an array of colored underpants. Kelsie stared at the mess for a moment and then, looking up at Bart, said, "I think you need a brand-new bag."

"Right," said Bart. "Kelsie, I like to think I'm donating

because it's the right thing to do, because Higg needs a kidney to save his life."

She gave him one of those "come off it" looks, but said only "Well, that's a reason."

"And, yes," said Bart, "I'd like to think Birdie, eh Mrs. Higgins, and I would still be friends after the donation. But if not, I think I will have done something good, or at least something useful, provided the old fart survives the operation."

"Which old fart are we talking about?"

"The other old fart."

Kelsie laughed.

The clothing filled sixteen large black trash bags and took most of the afternoon to pack and transport. Bart thanked Kelsie and made a date to have lunch sometime. She gave Bart a Fashion Faire receipt for tax purposes and left the "value of donation" blank for Bart to fill in. When she had left, Bart vacuumed the closet and then called Sophie. "Did you tell Kelsie Dahlia about my kidney donation?"

"Yeah, I did. I was hoping she might talk you out of it. Since Mom died, we talk quite often. She always asks how I'm doing, checks on Tom and the kids. Makes the calls Mom used to."

"And I don't?"

"Well, you really don't check up on me in the same way. Usually, I check up on you. I do think if we lived closer, you might enjoy your grandchildren. As to Kelsie, she's an attractive, smart, bucks-up, unattached widow. If I had to have a stepmother, I would choose her, not some married woman who wants your body to keep her husband alive, though when I think about it, Kelsie might want your body, too, if you gave her a chance."

"Seems like you and Kelsie consider Mrs. Higgins the lady

of darkness."

"No, that's not true. She's a nice person who has done good things for you and for Mom. But she's married with a dying husband. I'd save Tom if he were dying, and I think she'll do the same for Higg. You're sacrificing yourself for her, and I'm afraid she's going to hurt you. Oh, she'll be grateful; she just won't be there. You'll be sitting in that big empty house thinking of what might have been. So, if I could stop you, I would. But, as you have made clear, it's your body, and you can do what you want with it. I'm just your daughter who loves you. In the meantime, think about Kelsie or maybe one of the widows at the Sycamores."

The call ended. Yeah, multiple flings. Birdie, Kelsie, widows—his own personal stable. They were all nice in their way, but Birdie wasn't for keeps and Kelsie? Kelsie the widow, the society matron, the role model? Not sure he wanted that kind of life. He wanted Birdie, the one he couldn't have. But of course, you always want what you can't have.

Annoyed, and weary from cleaning out the closet, he got Lily's leash off its brass hook and headed for the park. He did not see Granny T until it was too late, although he wondered how he had missed her. She was wearing a large purple straw hat decorated like something out of Carmen, and fluffy pink cotton bloomers.

"Bart," she said, "I see you spent the afternoon with Kelsie Dahlia. A date?"

Oh God, just what he needed. "No, Gladys, a donation of Mary's clothes. It's taken me three years to face cleaning things out. Some nice things there. You might want to check out Fashion Faire."

"Kelsie's nice," said Gladys, "and a widow." Probably a better choice for you, Bart, than a married woman with a sick husband."

"I suppose," said Bart. "But for the moment, I think I'll stick with Lily."

"You should at least wait until poor Higg is gone."

"Gladys, why don't you . . ." He stopped himself. "Gladys, whether Higg stays or leaves depends on Higg. I'll give him his transplant and whether he keeps his wife is up to him. You and Johnny may split before Higg and Birdie do. But I must tell you," he winked at her, "if I hustle you next, I won't be able to donate a kidney to Johnny."

Gladys stiffened. "Be as smug as you like, but don't say I didn't tell you so. You're going to get what you deserve." She turned and walked away.

Bart stood thinking for a moment, watched Granny flounce down the street. He wondered what he deserved.

Later that evening, Birdie came to the back door with half a blackberry pie. She handed him the pie, said "I can't stay. Duty calls." But Higg had followed her, and as she turned around to leave, she almost knocked him over. "No, don't leave," Higg said. "I just got here. Let's, the three of us, eat some pie."

Higg, gaunt and jaundiced, made his way to a faded yellow kitchen chair. "What shall we talk about? Maybe talk about duty?" he said.

Birdie lowered her head. No one spoke. Bart could hear faint sounds of the neighborhood, a distant voice, a dog barking.

"How much pie do you want Higg," said Bart?

"I want the whole thing before both of us, the pie and me, become green with mold. It's not that I'm ungenerous, it's just that I don't like to share my wife's cooking."

Birdie said, "Higg, it's not what you . . . "but he waived her to silence.

He pointed at the Christmas Cactus sitting on top of a cupboard. "Water will save that cactus, perhaps make it flourish and cover itself with pink blossoms; or the plant can decide it's tired of living in a pot and die whether I give it water or not. Plants do that. They live for a time and then die for reasons known only to them."

"And which are you," said Bart?

"No idea. I just came for the pie."

"Take it," said Bart. "It was yours to begin with."

"Yes, it was—to begin with." Higg arose with effort, took the half pie and, with the aid of countertops, steered toward the door. As he went out, he said, "I'll be at home--as always."

Birdie said, "I'm sorry, Bart. You didn't deserve that. He's angry—angry at me, angry at you, angry at where he finds himself. I can't blame him, and he needs me right now." She smiled. "Someday I would hope we could be together without causing pain." She began to cry, gave Bart's arm a squeeze, and left.

Bart sat thinking for several minutes, reviewing the scene in his head. He poured himself a large bourbon and retreated to the empty living room. He could see streetlights and the park across the street. Better for once to be hidden in fog. He had not caused Higg's cancer, nor damaged Higg's body. That train had long since left the station. But, oblivious and without concern, he had stolen Higg's happy ending.

Sleep proved elusive. Hours of darkness filled with images and fragments of thought, a night like a wound-up clock whose hands did not move. Again and again he stepped on Higg to reach Birdie.

Time restarted at first light. The images stopped; the feelings remained. Higg had taken a knee, chosen life. Bart would don his tarnished armor and, perhaps for a time, wear Birdie's colors on his shield. But this morning, with headache and dry mouth, he stood like someone accused in front of the bathroom mirror.

Feel good about this, Bart? What's your real motive?

You donated for Birdie, a married woman. Mary would have respected a decision to save Higg, but not your desire for Birdie. "Really, Bart," she would have said. "The wife of a dying man?"

He drank a full glass of water and went back to bed.

Half awake, he saw himself on a cold hospital slab, naked, surrounded by the smell of antiseptic and a masked doctor wearing green. With a flourish, the doctor sliced him open and cut away a part of his insides. Then, roaring in triumph, Birdie tore off her doctor's mask and held Bart's kidney aloft in her outstretched hand.

Maybe Kelsie and Granny T saw things clearly. He pictured Birdie and Higg together eating large pieces of apple pie. The smell of cinnamon filled the kitchen. They were laughing. "He's such a fool," they said. "We probably could get both kidneys if we wanted."

No, he didn't believe it. Birdie had always treated him with kindness, even before Higg's kidney had failed. He remembered the many times she had come over—to help with Mary, to look after him. No, he didn't believe it.

Lily's barking awakened him. Now soundly asleep, Bart jumped into an awake darkness. He got up, saw Birdie standing at the kitchen door. Something must have happened to Higg.

"He's asleep," she said. He won't wake up until 9:00 am at the earliest. I need to talk to you."

"Sure. . . You want some coffee or something to eat?

"No, I can't stay long, just want to talk. I have a confession to make, and I wanted to tell you before you heard it from someone else. He took her into the living room and sat beside her. She said, "I've volunteered for years at the Blood Bank."

"I know that," he said.

"And I've known your blood type for a long time. I've known from the beginning you could be a donor for Higg. "

Bart looked at her, said nothing.

"But until you offered to Higg, I never thought of you as a donor. I thought of you as a friend and then, as you know, more than a friend. I would like to share your bed and your life. But I married Higg, and I'm killing him. I set out to save his life and now I take it. I can't do it. He's not without feeling. God knows he's been good to me. Honored me. Loved me."

They looked at each other in silence. Bart smiled, a sad smile, and slowly nodded his head. She was telling him goodbye.

"I want the transplant. I want life for Higg, though I'll understand if you decide not to donate. I want to package our feelings for each other and hold them close and safe. And I want you to walk away from me and untie the package from time to time and smile and cry. I need to end the Thursday night visits, end the piano lessons. I need to end Bart and Birdie."

"Ouch" His eyes filled with tears and then he took her in his arms and held her as long as he could. "I can't stay," she said, "or I won't leave." She left the kitchen and walked across the damp field. When she arrived, Higg was waiting at the door. "You look like you've been crying. Did you end it?"

"It never really started, Higg. But yes, I did. I'll miss him. He was my friend and support."

Ch 35. The Visit

72 degrees and sunny. A warm October day interrupted only by occasional bursts of cold wind. Nate had called an hour ago. "On his way," he said. Meanwhile Bart emptied Lily and then played ball with her until she refused to bring it back. He could see Higg across the field. He sat on his white plastic chair outside the piano room. Bart thought of yelling, "How's Birdie?", but he just waved.

Bart saw Amy the instant Nate parked. What had Nate done? Fifty years ago he had planned his life with Amy. Fifty years ago she had left without explanation. She had hurt him, and the hurt had never left. And fifty years ago he had put his feelings in a tight little box and kept them there. Now the box had opened. He did not know how to see her again.

Bart held onto his porch rail and watched. Amy, dressed in a dark blue pant suit—power clothes thought Bart-- still tall, slender, with the liquid body of an athlete. Some grey in her hair, but otherwise Amy, the brash, energetic, woman he had known and loved. Bart watched her confident exit from Nate's black Suburban, but then, perhaps uncertain like him, she stopped and fussed with her clothes. She had yet to see Bart.

Lily started to bark and gave the game away. Too late now to run. Too late to leave a note and the keys with Birdie. What had Nate done? Bart walked to the car.

"Dad, this is Amy."

"Oh, my God," said Bart, "back from the dead." But he knew she was never dead. He was the one who had died.

"No, just back for a night, if you'll have me."

"Well, until you leave again. Business trip? Visit to friends?"

She smiled. "No, Mr. Jones, I came to see you. Recruited by your son."

"Ah yes, him. You've come to rescue me from folly and imminent death."

"No, I've come to see you while you're still alive. And you're very much alive. In fact, you don't look a day over 80."

"Thanks," he said. "And you still look like Amy. Forever young." Now close to her, her lavender scent brought back their college apartment, board and brick bookcases, vinyl records, the unmade bed with its blue sheets and beige blanket. He had felt a sense of commitment when Amy had bought the bedding. At the time, it had scared him. And now she stood in front of him, and he didn't know how to act or what to say. He retreated to the obvious. "So how are you? And where have you been for 40 years?"

"Well, as your son would say, I've been studying dead Greeks. I found them more interesting than live men. Given my many accomplishments and awards, I honor you with my presence." She smiled a little too brightly. "I am honored," said Bart. "If I had a fatted calf, I would slaughter it."

It was close to lunch. Making the best of it, Bart took everyone to a favorite restaurant, the "Wheeler Inn". Mediocre food, but Bart liked the name. The Wheeler Inn, a retro restaurant, occupied a white corner building once named the San Sebastian Therapy and Rehabilitation Center. It now had juke boxes at Formica tables and 1940s uniformed servers.

"What do you recommend," asked Amy?

""It's basically a canned fruit-salad restaurant: the cherries taste the same as the grapes. Order anything on the menu. Your eyes will tell you what you're eating."

Amy put her hand on Bart's arm. "I was sorry to hear of the death of your wife. Having lost my husband, I know how difficult that is. They tell you to get out, develop new interests, start a love life."

He felt like a character in a play reading where actors

spoke according to script— "[move stage left] Sorry to hear about your wife, concerned about you, etc." "Amy, I had a wonderful 40 years, happy times, money, great children." He glanced at Nate. "Well at least one of them. Those years won't come back, but I'm not ready to pack it in." He studied her. "As to starting a love life, did you have something in mind?"

"Of course. I wanted to know if you were living again. I do remember parts of your love life, but I've been away for a few years."

"Yes, you vanished into the night, as I recall." Bart's response upset him. She's made an effort to come here, I can at least be polite.

He said, "But you're here now. And I'm happy for that. As to my love life, you remember the Woody Allen movie, the one where Gene Wilder falls in love with a sheep?"

"I do. 'Everything You Always Wanted to Know about Sex,' I think. Does that describe you?"

"No," said Bart with a straight face. "It has nothing to do with me." Everyone laughed. "These days I'm just a watcher at the pond. Lots of fantasies."

Nate interrupted. "Lots of opportunities. One's just unavailable."

Amy looked to Bart for an answer, but Bart just frowned.

"He's hot for his neighbor's wife," said Nate.

Bart glared at Nate. "Oh, for God's sake.

"My neighbor," said Bart, "has a sick husband. Several years ago I had a sick wife. During Mary's illness, the neighbor, Mrs. Higgins, came over, brought food, was there for me when I needed a friend. Now she talks to me about her husband. I listen and try to be there for her."

"You also take piano from her," said Nate.

"Yes, thanks to you and Sophie, but it's the same thing. We

talk about her husband when we're not talking about keeping my thumbs off the black keys."

"I don't believe it," said Nate. "The husband's a complete cipher. You can't stand him, and I'm not sure she can either."

"And how does that affect you, Nate? No, don't answer that. Higg's not a cipher. He's just a complete engineer. I don't share his interests. And, while we're turning over rocks, I don't share his wife—except to hear about her husband's medical problems."

"But," said Amy, "as I understand it, you intend to donate a kidney to this 'cipher' despite the strenuous opposition of your family." She laughed, "How can we, you and I, start up again if you're dead?"

Bart looked perplexed at first, then started laughing, which soon infected the entire table. When he could breathe again, he raised a hand calling for quiet. Then in a calm voice he said, "I've decided not to die--at least not any time soon. And I don't have any significant relationship with Mrs. Higgins, or her husband for that matter. And if I wanted her, I wouldn't be saving him. The doctors gave him six months to live without a transplant. Most of that time has passed."

"So why are you doing this," said Amy? "Who are you doing this for?"

"I think I'm doing it for me. I think I'm doing it because it's the right thing to do. As for my love life, who knows? Someday I'll go fishing and find a cod who's trustworthy and interested in an ocean-going trout."

"If you live."

"Yes, if I live."

After lunch, back at the house, Amy took a nap. Nate left to visit friends; said he would not return until the next day. Bart took Lily for a long walk, hoping to sort out the afternoon. He didn't know whether to disinherit Nate or thank him. As to

Amy . . .

Later, Bart sat opposite the couch where Amy, always confident and self-assured, enjoyed the sunset and sipped a glass of rosé. She talked of the Second Peloponnesian War, lectured to Bart as if he were an undergraduate. Still attractive though, thought Bart, lithe, sexy. He remembered how she used to tease him, display her body and beckon him while holding him at arm's length. The memory captured him, until, with a start, Amy knocked over her wine glass yanking Bart back into the present. Maybe she was having the same thoughts. He almost laughed out loud. He cleaned up, salted the rug where she had spilled the wine, refilled her glass. Embarrassed, she continued with Classics 101, but now fidgeted while she talked. Talked with her hands.

Amy still attracted him, even as she recounted her career, her studies, her travels. He did enjoy her, but he should probably forget the past. He'd been burned once, but that didn't mean it would happen again. He thought of his father's adage about a cat. 'A cat that jumps on a hot stove will not jump on a hot stove again. But it also will not jump on a cold one.' Maybe he was the cat.

The kitchen door opened with a squeak. A light went on. Bart? Bart, are you decent? I've brought a pie."

Bart shook his head in disbelief. What next? Bart said, "I'm always decent. Come into the living room. I'd like you to meet someone. He turned on the overhead light. "Birdie, I'd like you to meet Amy Rice, now Amy Echlin. We were students together at Stanford. Amy lost her husband at about the same time I lost Mary. Nate brought her down here for the weekend. Amy was just regaling me about Greek warfare, her area of expertise.

"Birdie is my special neighbor who has watched over me since before Mary died. Her kindness has kept me going."

Each woman measured the other. The academic, slender

with the physique of a runner; the homemaker—athletic, broad shouldered. Both smiled in that customary false delight of greeting a rival, somewhat like two lions meeting over an antelope.

Amy said, "I envy your skill in baking pies. With my career, I never got past Top Ramen. Fortunately, my husband was an excellent cook."

"I'm not sure I'm skilled at baking. I just try to keep Bart happy. Anyway I can't stay. My husband's not doing well. I'll see myself out." She kissed Bart on the cheek and left.

Amy said, "She seems like a nice person. Too bad she's married."

Ten minutes later they called it a night. Bart showed Amy the guest bedroom and bath. Said, "If you need anything, I'm right down the hall."

Bart retreated to his room with an uncertain smile like an unsigned all-star fought over by the Yankees and the Dodgers. Amy, Birdie: the returned lover; the still warm feeling of Birdie's kiss. And if Amy, just down the hall, should call for his help? Better to think about his imaginary cruise and the lady from Morgantown.

Nate returned the next morning. Cold, foggy. Found his dad out with the dog. "Don't ever do that to me again," said Bart. "I'm your father, not one of your fucking clients." He walked back into the house. Nate, like a scolded puppy, followed his father tail down into the house.

They found Amy drinking tea next to her overnight case. She said, "Time to go, I guess." She gave Bart a big, too-long hug. "Goodbye, Bart," she said. "I'll see you again. I know I hurt you when I left. I hurt myself too. I'm sorry."

Alone in the car, Nate said, "Well?"

"He's got the same charm. It's like I never left. I can feel myself getting sucked in already. But he's afraid of me. I'm not sure he'd ever trust me—that is, if he lives and I get the chance. But I do have a solution for the kidney donation. Call it payback for putting me into this situation.

"Really. What's that?"

"You donate a kidney in his place."

Ch 36. Travel

Fortunately, Nate's trip to the airport was short and the conversation with Amy minimal. Amy played the role of adult mixed with a slight amount of condescension, somewhat like an older sister. At the airport she hugged him. Told him things would work out.

He watched her stride through security and waved. Well, Mrs. Lincoln, aside from that, how did you like the play? He was batting 1000. His dad was pissed and dug in, Amy treated him like a misbehaving child, and he still had to talk with Sophie. One thing at a time. Probably Dad and Sophie in that order.

Nate bought a coffee at Peet's and established himself opposite baggage carousel #3. He got out his laptop, suppressed his gag reflex, and started to write.

> Dad, I want to apologize for this weekend. I was wrong. Wrong in finding Amy, a source of your hurt, and putting her back into your life. Wrong in thinking your life was my life. What you do with your life, your body, is your business. Am I concerned about the outcome of your decision to donate? Of course. Both Sophie and I, in our own ways, have tried to talk you out of it. I won't meddle further, but I love you and am here for you if you need me.
>
> Nate
>
> P.S. I found Amy impressive and alluring. I can understand your loss.

He leaned back from the computer, decided to let the email sit for a while before sending it. Maybe he would think of something on his drive north.

Traffic on Highway 101 was slow. He called Sophie from the car and told her what he had done.

"Oh, Jesus, Nate. You've got to be kidding."

"Hey, someone wanted my help because they struck out. I tried to show him what he could lose. You should meet Amy."

Sophie mumbled something Nate didn't understand and

then said, "When I think about it, an indirect approach was all we had left. I failed with a direct plea, and he doesn't listen to you. So I apologize. Sorry I got angry. Does Mrs. Higgins know of the risk he takes?" Nate had no idea. "I think I might find out," she said.

Continuing his drive, Nate wondered about Amy's suggestion that he donate in place of his father. He thought at first she made the comment in jest, but began to think perhaps she was serious. The idea didn't appeal to him, but he hadn't really thought about it. He did imagine his rock climbing, snowboarding, and playing back for his rugby club would be "inadvisable" with one kidney, plus he hated hospitals.

Maybe a surrogate? What would a kidney cost and how fast could it be arranged? A potential donor would need a thorough medical and background check, assuming he could find one. Timing probably would be the biggest factor, not to mention the expense. And he wasn't sure all that could be done in time to save Higg. Of course, he didn't think Higg had much to do with it. More likely, Dad thinking with his small brain. And as to Dad's health, no doctor would perform this operation if it would endanger Dad—especially not on a retired lawyer.

He could offer to donate just to show his concern, maybe earn some points with Dad, make Amy and Sophie happy. But making such an offer to Dad made him shudder. He'd need asbestos earmuffs and a shield.

No, it wouldn't work. Dad wouldn't consent; there was not enough time to find and qualify a replacement. So, relieved, Nate turned off onto the 280 freeway thinking of cold cracked crab, an artichoke, and a nice dry Riesling. He wondered if he had enough mayonnaise for the artichoke or should stop and get some. Probably not worth the effort. He could always use butter.

◆ ◆ ◆

It took Amy longer to get her car from long-term parking than to fly from SBP to SFO. Fortunately, at San Francisco, she had taken a picture of her parking space. She expected to feel stressed, exhausted from the weekend, but instead felt renewed, as if someone had opened the door to sunshine and the smell of mountain air. She had not lost her feelings for Bart.

When she arrived home, as a thank you, she had a note and a bottle of wine delivered to Bart's house. The note read:

Dear Bart,

I enjoyed our meeting, albeit short, and I enjoyed us. In many ways, it was as if I had never left. Thank you for hosting me, for your toleration and for your forgiveness. I would like to see you again.

With love,

Amy

P.S. Please don't be too hard on Nate. He is concerned for you and was trying to do the right thing. Besides, in some respects, he could be your clone.

Ch 37. Come to Jesus

On Monday morning, still smarting from Nate's "reintroduction" of Amy, Bart sat in his living room listening to the quiet morning. The fog had lifted, and sun shone at the edges of the pulled blinds creating yellow streaks on the mantel and its family pictures. After about ten minutes and some restful breathing, Bart called Nate and Sophie. Talking on speaker, he began without small talk. "I felt embarrassed and humiliated this last weekend. I'm still angry. It felt more like an intervention than a visit, as if I had a serious problem that I refused to recognize. And to compound matters, you went outside the family for help with your poor weak father who could not or would not help himself."

Nate interrupted, "Well, you're about to do something stupid and you won't talk with us. It's as if we don't exist. I got Amy as a last resort to get your attention. And I got it. And I don't think you hated the weekend as much as you're making out. But have it your way. I'm sorry, Dad, I blew it."

"My God, Nate, you not only invited her, but you also put her in the bedroom down the hall from me. And I was to do what, tell her she couldn't stay and needed to find a motel room? Or was I supposed to sneak down the hall and hop her? But Sophie doesn't get a pass. You're both in this together."

"Sophie didn't know anything about this until after I did it."

What a far cry from when they were young. In those days, they couldn't wait to hang each other out. Now Nate's falling on his sword. "She still doesn't get a pass. As far as I can tell, your actions stem from one afternoon where you, Nate, decided I had become a recluse, holed up in my compound waiting for the FBI to burn it down. But, if you had thought about it, my wife had just died after 40 years of marriage. My full house had turned into a pair of threes overnight, and after receiving the sympathy of every relative I never knew we had, I was left alone with Lily and that wonderful cat of your mom's, who, knowing I'd put him in the nearest coin-op dryer, had the grace to split."

Both kids talked at once. "Dad, we thought. . . I'm sorry." Bart raised his voice.

"The two of you didn't realize, and still don't realize, that you don't transition from married to single overnight— especially not after living together for almost a half a century. I know you want to help, but you don't have a dog in this fight, at least not a big dog. Whether I change or don't change depends on me, on Bartholomew Jones. And whether I go out, stay in, greet Jehovah's Witnesses naked at my front door—is beyond your control. Yes, I recognize you care about me, and I care about you. But as long as I'm not hurting anyone, except perhaps religious solicitors, I get to call the shots."

Sophie said, "We thought you were hurting yourself, thought you had given up, watched you sit in the house in front of the TV. That's why we wanted to get you reengaged, maybe move to a retirement community where you'd have . . ." There was shouting in the background. ". . . people around. We. . . OK, just settle down." She shouted at her kids. "Both of you go to your rooms. Now!" Bart could feel their retreat. Sophie said, "I'm sorry. Anytime we get into a serious conversation, they act out. "

"Have you tried beatings?" said Nate.

"No, the next step is to send them to you."

"Let's go on," said Bart. He blew out a breath and then in a measured voice said. "I appreciate, I have appreciated your concern—and your love. But I don't appreciate your judging me using your 40-year-old lifestyles as the standard of normal behavior. I ran out of steam after the ordeal with your mother, but I haven't lost it simply because I'm no longer riding an 850-pound Harley and running marathons. And I've yet to pee in a potted plant." Probably, he thought, because they're no potted plants around. "And I'm not dying of loneliness because I talk to you on the phone occasionally. And finally, yes, I know you disagree with my decision to donate a kidney, but it's my body and my decision. In summary, I appreciate your concerns, value your input, but you're not my parents. I would like your support and your blessing, but I don't need your consent."

There was silence on the other end of the line. He hoped he had not gone too far.

"Can I talk," said Sophie?

"Sure, go ahead. I've said what I wanted to say—which is, give me some credit for having an ounce of intelligence. Recognize I'm not your young jock father and at 68, I might have different interests and different views of life and living."

Both kids started talking at once with Nate finally prevailing. "Dad, after Mom died, you went from active to stone, sitting in front of a TV. Never in your life had you been so inactive. And you did it for two years. You stopped seeing people and sat around and got fat."

"I did not get fat."

Sophie said, "And this was the dad who loved change, who reinvented himself every five years. First an avid cyclist, biking centuries and riding up and down Highway 1. Nepenthe, Kirk Creek, Hearst Castle. In fact I rode the last one down from Carmel with you. Then, along with running 30+ miles per week, you became Mr. Wilderness and spent a month and a half every summer in the Sierra climbing peaks and living under a shelter half. You were fond of saying, 'Trees just obstruct the view.'"

"Yeah Sophie, but. . . "

"I'm not done. And along the way you rode the largest motorcycles you could find and drove your latest hot car up Highway 1 at first light so you could speed at 100 miles an hour and avoid the Highway Patrol. And you kept up with your backpacking and running until Mom got sick. And then you quit. Just quit. Quit everything as far as we could tell. We found you treading water, sitting on the couch looking like Jabba the

Hutt. We didn't want to change you. We wanted to restore you, reconnect you, move you."

Nate started to say something, but apparently thought better of it. Sophie didn't need any help. He said, "I can't take that call right now" to someone.

Bart said, "As I remember, I ran a marathon at age 64 and a couple of halves after that. And you left out my flying and playing trombone. But as far as moving me, I think you two have succeeded. You've certainly got my attention."

"Thank you," said Nate.

"Yeah, I haven't watched Days of Our Lives in almost a week. Seriously, I do thank you for your efforts. But let's call a truce. I'm your father, not your child. The Amy stunt was way over the top. And you've beaten the kidney to death. In fact, I now may have only one healthy kidney and can no longer donate.

"I admit, I have had fun with Dr. James and have learned a lot about myself. As to piano lessons. . . well, we shall see. So I thank you both for all your efforts, but now let's call it a day. You don't get to be my parents until I'm 90 or maybe 95."

"Do we still get to be your children?"

"Of course."

"I'm sorry" said Sophie, "I left out the flying and the trombone."

They ended the call with forgiveness all around. All's well that ends well, thought Bart. Why do I feel like a raft adrift at sea?

Ch 38. Frank

Bart looked around Dr. James' waiting room, noticed *Bringing a Pet Pig into Your Home* missing from the bookcase. Well it stayed there longer than I expected. Who knows? Maybe someone bought a pig.

Called into the inner sanctum, Bart recited the events of the previous 24 hours starting with semi-naked Kelsie in Mary's hot closet and her warning about Birdie, followed by Granny T wearing pajamas on the street and her warning about Birdie; Higg's silent challenge of the Birdie and Bart relationship; and Birdie's ending that relationship at a secret 2:00 am visit.

"Then, at some ungodly hour," said Bart, "after my terrific evening and a night from hell, Higg presents himself at my kitchen door. The color of a week-old lemon, he looks like he's already died. He hangs on my kitchen counter and pleads in between sobs: 'I forced her to give up a friend,' he says, 'to give up her shoulder and support during all these troubles with me, and I cut the rug from under her; I was selfish and did not think. She needs you, Bart, she needs you to be there for her. Please, please forgive me.'"

"What did you do?"

"I raised him up, held him, put my arm around his shoulder—told him everything would be OK. Then I took him home. I didn't know what else to do. Sitting here in this office, I can still hear his sobs, his begging for forgiveness.

Anyway, "I've gone full circle in 24 hours. I've been hit on, warned, confronted, dumped, apologized to, and reinstated."

"And are you happy?"

"No. I want to know where my pig book went."

The doctor pulled open a desk drawer. "It's right here. Too many questions about my intent and its therapeutic purpose." He smiled. "Thanks by the way.

"Getting back to your 24 hours, has it changed your mind about making the donation?"

"No"

"About Birdie?"

"I suppose you could argue Birdie's termination of 'us' could validate Kelsie and Granny T's warnings. But I think she acted honestly. I don't know what to think about my reinstatement. I guess I'm reinstated, but I've only talked with Higg."

"But you're still OK with the donation?"

"It's the right thing to do."

"Yeah, but there's gotta be something behind the right."

"The guy dies without a transplant. That's not right enough?"

"So you feel sorry for him."

"I feel sorry for Birdie." Bart started to ask a question, and then stopped, got up and took off his coat.

"But you don't know why he wants to live or how he feels about things. Have you talked with him?"

Bart exhaled, mumbled to himself, "Is this therapy or interrogation?" Then smiling, but looking a bit exasperated, said, "Doctor, I've talked with him four times now, though I'm not sure I know his feelings. Before my 'reinstatement', I thought I knew where his head was. Higg, as you know, refused my offer and then changed his mind. He refused at first I think, because it showed me as a good guy, put him in my debt. Later he thought about it, realized if he died I got the girl, so he changed his mind. If I underwent the procedure, he would get the kidney, keep the girl, wink at me and wave goodbye. He might still die, but he'd have the last laugh. I think he still feels the same way about me, but he's realized Birdie needs a friend, maybe something more if he dies.

"So Mr. Cynic, why give him a kidney? Do nothing and get the girl."

"Well for starters, I made the offer, and it would be rather cruel to hang him out at this point. He'll die without my kidney, and maybe will die with it. Anyway, that ship's left the dock."

Bart pursed his lips. "How about guilt, Doctor? He's dying and I've stolen his wife. Does that work for you?"

"It's a reason."

"But to be honest, I just wanted to do the right thing. Try this: My offer resulted from innate ethical knowledge. It was my ineffable response to the needs of a dying person."

"Oh, please." The doctor opened his hand as if to waive, "OK, let's get practical. Have you ever discussed the donation with Birdie? For example, have you discussed the dangers of this procedure with her?"

"My doctors have OK'd my donating".

"I thought your doctors advised against it—something about crashing helicopters and motorcycles."

"Well I'm not running marathons these days. But they've consented, and I think I'll live. Bottom line, I told her I would donate. And no, I haven't discussed the dangers of the procedure with her."

"If she knew there were a danger to you, would she support the donation?"

"I don't know. I know she wants to save Higg. If she thought I might die. . . "

"She would be conflicted."

"Yeah, I think so, hope so at least."

Bart yawned, looked at his watch. 10 minutes. He had only been here 10 minutes. The discussion seemed repetitive and endless. He had committed to donate a kidney and had offered various honest reasons for his decision. None had satisfied the doctor. He probably should man up and just ask the doctor what answer he wanted because at the moment they were stuck in a loop tape. 40 more minutes 'til lunch. He'd hit La Casita today and go to the park afterward. A bit of a drive, but he liked the food. And Lily would like the park.

"Bart," said the doctor?

"Sorry. I tuned out. Maybe you could repeat your last question."

"Have you thought about Birdie's feelings?"

"I know she's concerned about Higg, but if I'm comfortable with myself, with my decision to donate. Why would I want to share her feelings? To solve a problem or predict behavior, I can understand your wanting to know where someone is coming from. But share their feelings? You don't feel what I feel. You're a trained psychiatrist. Day to day you look at patients driving off the road or veering in that direction, and you try to correct them. That's your job. But you don't suffer the driver's pain when they turn toward a tree. You can't. You'd lose your objectivity. You'd lose the ability to evaluate and counsel your patient. Given the choice, you're not going to share pain." Bart looked at the doctor with raised eyebrows. "Well?"

"Look, just bear with me for a while; I think you might find it useful. Tell me about Higg. What's he feeling?"

Bart moaned. Beating a dead horse came to mind. "Higg faces death. He may be feeling sorry for himself, concerned about Birdie, humiliated by me, or wondering what it would feel like to hop in the sack with Gladys Tharp. I really don't know. After I restored my offer, I would guess he's feeling relieved but feeling humiliated at the same time. But so what? I've offered to donate. He's accepted. Why do I care?

"Have you ever 'been there' when a client died?"

"Yes, several times. One you've heard: The death of Billy's

mother, Susan. I was also present at the death of Frank. Not my client. I was a witness to his will."

"When we talked about Susan, Jack and Billy," said Dr. James, "we focused on Billy and not on Susan. Tell me about Frank and your memory of his death. Try remembering your feelings."

Bart just shook his head, started to laugh. "You're not going to let this go, are you?"

Dr. James, looking innocent, said "No."

"OK, I'll tell you Frank's story, and what he said to me several minutes before he died. When I'm done, we can talk about my feelings. You can hold my hand and share my pain."

Dr. James closed his notebook and put notebook and pen on the desk. "Fine," he said, "tell me the story."

"I think we need a break first," said Bart. He got up, stretched, and fetched two bottles of water from the doctor's fridge. After a long drink, he began. "I'd heard about Frank for years. When I finally met him, he was pushing 80. Holed up in his run-down house, he only went out once a week or so to buy food. Neighbor lady took him.

"He was beyond cheap. This was a guy with money who showed up at the food bank for what he described as "give-away-cheese." In his driveway sat the rusted-out hulk of his Cadillac, undriven for years, pale blue with white interior and fins. It was at least 100 feet long."

Bart sat up in his chair, continued. "Well everyone knew Frank had money. And so Frank had 'friends' who did things for him from time to time—fixed the toilet, repaired a screen— things like that. Frank also had a daughter. Don't remember her name. She visited once a year or so, maybe not all that often. And Frank had Elsie, or vice versa.

"Elsie served as the minder of the town's old men. In fact she had somewhat of a stable. When they no longer could take care of themselves, she moved them into her house, fed and cooked for them. When they died, out of gratitude I'm sure, they always left her a 'little something.' Not enough to cause a ruckus, or a will contest, but enough to provide a bit for her care and support. Frank lived several doors down from Elsie and had his own house. Elsie looked after Frank there."

"Go on," said the doctor.

"Like everyone else in our small town, I had known Elsie for years as the ever-present waitress in the town's only café, Egdon Hearth. Small, hardy, always cheerful, Elsie had the perfect soft skin of a baby that did not show her 70 plus years. Elsie knew everyone; everyone knew Elsie.

"One morning, after hot biscuits and sausage gravy—I didn't watch my cholesterol in those days—Elsie asked me if I would witness a will signing, and, in a moment of weakness or stupidity or both, I said yes. Another attorney in town represented Frank and had prepared the will. I just had to show up and sign. We were to meet at 2:00 that afternoon.

"When I arrived, Elsie was eating her lunch and Mrs. Stevens, a lady from down the street, sat in a living room chair. She would be the second witness. Elsie said Frank was sleeping and did not want to wake him. I declined coffee or a snack.

"'He never sleeps long,' Elsie said. He'll be awake in ten minutes.' In the meantime, she held the remains of cold fried chicken on her plate, and gnawed and plucked bits from the carcass until it looked like an oak tree in winter. She then wiped the grease from her hands, and fetched a bunch of green grapes from the kitchen. These she jerked one by one, popping each grape into the rapid clack of her dentures.

"'You know,' she said, 'I've taken care of Frank for five years now. She pulled off a grape and began to chew. He's got a daughter. She never visits and when she does, takes everything that's not nailed down.' She pulled off another grape. 'Frank said he's remembered me for all I done for him. I got that attorney

Clinton to write a will for him. Only cost eighty bucks. But Frank never signed it. And then. . .'

"With her rapid nervous talk and noise of her eating, after a time I tuned her out and just nodded. I was not feeling good about things.

"After about ten minutes or so, Frank woke up. Elsie went into the bedroom, and I remember some raised voices. I suppose they were 'sharing feelings'. Anyway, Elsie soon emerged from the bedroom and said Frank would sign.

"Mrs. Stevens and I found Frank in bed, obviously weak and sick. I got Elsie to leave the room and asked Frank about his family. He said he had a daughter and told us her name. Although he was not my client, I read the will to him. He said it was OK with him. Told us he was leaving something to Elsie and the rest to his daughter. He asked if she had come. Said he hadn't seen her for a while, but he was sure she would show up to get whatever she could. Said she and Elsie would have a good time in the ring together. Sorry he was going to miss it.

"After the signing, the 'execution' in legal terms, Mrs. Stevens left, and I let Elsie back into the room. She didn't even see me. To this day, I can still see her standing there with the plucked grape stem in her hand."

Dr. James said, "So Frank, on his deathbed, wanted to see the fight between Elsie and his daughter—the neighbor eager for 'a little something', the daughter who only visited to get what she could. How do you think Frank felt?"

"I think he felt alone."

"And how did that make you feel?"

Bart could see Frank propped up in his bed, looking at him through watery eyes. "I got choked up, wanted to reach out to him, keep him from going away by himself. I remember taking his hand, putting my other hand on his shoulder. A half hug I guess. I couldn't do much else." Bart sat back, rested a hand on the doctor's desk.

"So you shared his feelings. And did it matter?"

"I didn't share his feelings. I identified his feelings and tried to comfort him. But yes, it mattered to both of us. Frank lay in his bed dying, an abandoned old man traveling solo without friend or family. But, when I think about it, death always travels solo.

"And yes, the experience stayed with me. I can still see Frank, still see the room and the bed, hear his rough breathing, smell the disinfectant. But I can't feel for everyone—especially as a professional. And I don't think you can either. You can recognize feelings, must recognize feelings. Call it 'rational empathy' if you will. But, bottom line, as a lawyer and as a psychiatrist as well, you're hired to think, not to feel. You wouldn't last long if you felt for everyone."

"I suppose", said Dr. James, "we're talking about a duty or motivation to act. What must you do once you recognize a person's feelings? Is there some duty or moral obligation, beyond your professional responsibility, to go beyond recognition?"

"If you're like me," said Bart, "you might feel obligated to do the right thing. . . or not."

After another half hour of conversation, the session ended. Neither Dr. James nor Bart changed their positions.

After lunch and somewhat tired from the morning, Bart drove to the park, wanting to walk and think. The day, overcast and on the cool side, kept the park free of pedestrians. A few people with dogs, an occasional runner but none of the "walk-100-feet-and-sit-on-the-bench" set. Men worked shovels and hot asphalt, "improving" parts of the main trail. Others pruned shrubs that obscured a flower bed.

Bart wasn't sure what Dr. James wanted. Yes, he knew the difference between sympathy and empathy. But share people's feelings? How many client deaths could he have shared until he shared his own? He hadn't liked the questions, the prodding, the insinuation that if you helped someone but didn't participate in their grief, you weren't a good person. He had liked the shrink sessions when he began and had learned something about himself. Certainly he became aware of how he used humor. But lately these meetings had become tiresome. Maybe time to give it a rest.

White barricades now lined the trail. Workers had dug up a green lawn and were putting some type of equipment in the middle. A sign read, "A Measure Y Park Improvement Project." I like the park as is, thought Bart. Can't they just leave it alone?

He thought of Amy, brought to him by his only son, who thought what? Dad will find something to live for and rethink this stupid transplant? Amy was indeed still Amy. Sexy, brash, alluring. But a stranger. He no longer knew her. She was an attractive 68-year-old woman who shared his bed 45 years ago. Take up where they left off? Nice thought—especially the sex.

He also didn't trust her. Would he fall in love only to wake up one morning to an empty bed? Easy to overlay the past on the present, but to be fair, the past doesn't usually govern the present. Yes, Amy had left him long ago, but that did not mean she would leave him today.

He had looked at what happened in the past only from his viewpoint. She was not impulsive, nor was she fickle or irrational. She could not, for her own reasons face him, explain why she intended to leave. As she said, she hurt herself as well as him. That she had agreed to come back now, to see him again, showed courage and humility.

He should write to her and apologize for his behavior.

Explain if he could. He also had treated Nate too roughly. Both Nate and Sophie had convinced themselves he would die as a result of this operation. He didn't think so, but he honestly wouldn't know until it finished. And if it finished too soon, he wouldn't know at all.

Ch 39. Reconciliation

Tuesday Evening

On Tuesday evening Bart built a fire, settled into his giant chair, and attempted to read. His mind was elsewhere. The nice thing about kidney donations, aside from getting the family on your case, the threat of death and all that, is separation. The donor and donee need not hold hands and sing Kumbaya but can go forward separately. The paperwork must meet, but the participants need not. Goodbye, Higg.

Scheduling the procedure had had its challenges—mainly, to find an available doctor who could perform the procedure. Higg's urologist was out of the country and not expected to return for several months. Other doctors typically responded with remote dates: "The doctor has an opening the next winter solstice, but we might be able to fit you in earlier if there's a cancellation." However, after some effort, mainly on the part of Birdie, mercy prevailed. The procedure would take place on Wednesday. Bart would tell the kids after it was over. They could do nothing anyway.

As to outcomes, his doctors had told Bart he most likely would survive the procedure but, because of his age, would face a longer period of recovery. Birdie knew the schedule and would drive him to the hospital. He expected she would be there at the finish, but if not, there was always Lyft.

In the meantime, Bart wanted to make amends. Setting his book aside, he first wrote to Amy and apologized for his behavior. Said please judge him by the second half of her visit, not the first. Told her he would like to see her again. He then wrote to Nate. Said, "Don't sweat it. You were trying to do the right thing. I'll get over it. Hope you don't mind the changes to my trust."

After a while he could read no longer and went to bed. He had been asleep for a couple of hours when he heard soft steps in the room. Awake, frightened at first, he watched Birdie move across the room and slip into bed alongside him. As he started to talk, she put a finger to his lips. "Shhh. Just let me hold you. I don't know what will happen on Wednesday or whether we'll be together again. Higg will need special care. And I'm his wife. I'll do what I must. But for now let's be together while we can. Hold me and let me love you. Maybe, as they say, tomorrow will never come.

In quiet nights, alone in his big house, Bart had dreamed this moment. Birdie in his bed, her body smelling fresh and bathed, her wonderful strength and warmth. He had dreamed of her taste, her smell, the matching feeling of bare skin. All these dreams had now come true. He loved her as she loved him. Yet tonight frightened him. She was not his and would leave him before dawn. He told himself they would always have this night, this moment. But he would much rather have her.

Ch 40. Resurrection

One Week Later

This would be Bart's last shrink session for a while, at least until he got better or died. Bart said he would be a nicer person after the procedure because, with but a single kidney, he would be less pissed off. He said he would explain the stories of Elsie and Frank to Dr. James when he got back from the hospital, but in the meantime wanted to tell the doctor one last story, a story that might explain his behavior, but in any case, a story the doctor could ponder in the future until Bart returned. "When I finish the story," said Bart, "the session will end. I'll pay for whatever's left, whether my time is over or under."

The doctor nodded. "So you're going to pay to tell me a story. Fair enough. Maybe we both will learn something."

Bart motioned the doctor to a chair and cleared his throat. Held the side of the office table as if it were a lectern. "Pay attention now."

The doctor nodded.

"When our kids were teenagers, we vacationed in Mineral King, now part of Sequoia National Park. You get to Mineral King by driving up an exposed, narrow mountain road, about 20 miles in length, which climbs 7000 feet or so above the town of Three Rivers below. It's not a road for a flat-lander or someone who has a fear of heights. But in terms of beauty and breathtaking vistas, not to mention a challenging drive, the Mineral King Road offers a substantial reward.

Mineral King, named after the mines once inhabiting its slopes, consists of a pristine subalpine valley surrounded by jagged granite peaks, the most prominent of which is Sawtooth Peak at over 12,000 feet. The headwaters of the Kaweah River, bordered by willows, heather, and aspen, flow through the valley floor. As the valley increases in elevation, cedar, foxtail pine, and blue spruce predominate until tree line at about 9000 feet. "

"Tree line?"

"Where the trees end and the rock begins. Not much grows at the higher elevations. Anyway, that summer we stayed in Silver City, about the only non-camping place in the park. Silver City contains a restaurant and a collection of ancient wood cabins, most with outside decks, and all with character. We hiked, read, went for runs on the valley floor, basically got out of San Sebastian, hung out and soaked in the sun and surroundings.

"Nate and Sophie were both teenagers at the time, and, like Mary and me, both distance runners and experienced backpackers. And, as you might expect, after several days of hiking and reading, the kids wanted more challenging activities. We hadn't come equipped for backpacking, so I talked to the cowboys at the Mineral King Stable for advice. They suggested a guided trip by horseback from Mineral King Valley to the White Chief Mine. This abandoned mine, named after an Indian chief, hides in a remote canyon at around 10,500 feet and is accessed by a steep narrow trail. Nate quickly embraced the idea, and, after some hesitation Sophie said yes but wasn't sure about riding 3500 feet up a mountain trail. Mary, who did neither horses nor heights, said "No." She did not like the idea given our inexperience with horses on a mountain trail. We pointed out that we had a guide and would be riding with other inexperienced people. And these were stable horses, not some free-range stallions. She still didn't like it, but in the end did not stop us."

"I'm surprised your kids would go on such a vacation. Not sure reading and hiking would entice the modern teenager."

"Well, One, it was a different time, and Two, they had no choice.

"So, next day, we're at the stable on a bright crisp morning, along with 10 or so other people, where their staff fits and saddles each rider for a horse based on his or her size and riding experience. After all had mounted, Jeff, our guide, slim, rugged in dirty jeans and a sweat-stained cowboy hat, led us across the valley floor on a meandering trail through aspens, willows, and red fir. The trail was damp that morning, there was no dust, only the fresh early morning smell, as yet not stolen by the sun.

"My horse trod in a slow pace accompanied by the steady sound of its hooves, and I found myself soon in what could have been a dream. I still remember staring with fascination at the underside of the fir branches, their grey/green patterns intricate and geometric, as if designed by a master craftsman or weaver of fine lace. I lost myself in those trees, saw things that were always there, but I had never seen. For a time, I think I was part of their world." Bart shrugged, and then feeling embarrassed, said, "I don't know. Probably I'd just had too much wine to drink the night before.

"As we climbed out of the trees, the trail had turned rocky, narrow and exposed. The right side of the trail dropped off to a dry riverbed some 200 feet below, and in most places, only two feet separated the trail from the drop-off. Worse, a steep hillside blocked the left side of the trail. We rode single file up this rocky shelf with most places not wider than a horse. And my horse, I don't remember her name, changed at this point from hypnotic to a moving leather seat some five feet in the air." Bart shuddered. He could still see the narrow trail, and the drop-off, still feel the fear.

Gathering his thoughts, Bart said, "Basically, you couldn't go left, you could follow the trail, or you could go over a cliff to the right. I remembered telling myself, 'Horses have four legs and are sure footed.' But horses also follow their head. A rider moves the horses head with reins to control the direction of the horse. But when on a narrow trail with a drop-off on one side, a horse does not look straight ahead, it looks at the drop-off. The horse walks forward and follows the trail, but with its head turned to the edge of the drop-off, and you, the rider, feel, know, believe, that at any moment the horse, and you, will walk into space. And you wonder how you got here, and you want to get off the horse, but you can't and there's nothing you can do about but go forward.

"At last, a long hour after we had left the valley, we stopped at a small flat space between the trail and the drop off. There was, at last, some room to get off our horses, but not much. The steep hillside still blocked the left side of the trail, and the riverbed still lay 200 feet below on the right. There was barely enough space to dismount, but I was happy to get off the horse. I could crawl now if I had to, and yes, I thought about walking back down the mountain.

"Suddenly, Jeff began to shout. 'Oh, that's so great', he said, 'That's so good.' He raised both arms and clapped his hands over his head. 'She will not be wasted. She will live again.'

"Farther to the right, I heard Sophie crying, 'Oh, my God, Oh my God.' There was commotion among the horses, and at first, I could not see what had happened. And then I looked over the cliff edge. On the river bottom below lay a dead horse. A brown bear stood over the horse pulling out great strands of pink flesh, muscle. . . I don't know. It was the color of bubble gum. The guide was shouting, 'This is so great. She will live again.' And he was ecstatic and laughed and cried. The rest of us just stood and watched in horror. Took in a scene that would never leave us. To this day I can still see that pink color, and the horse, and the bear; feel the exposure of that trail and my helplessness.

"When Jeff stopped yelling, no one spoke. No one could speak. We were all frozen in place. Jeff then raised both arms in the air and called for quiet. I think he had seen our faces, maybe felt out reaction. 'Don't be scared,' he said. 'This is a good thing. You've are blessed to see this. The bear eating the horse is a good thing, a good thing. The horse has not gone to waste, but will be useful. She will live again in the bear.' He continued. 'Let me tell you about Josephine, tell you what happened here. Yesterday, I packed in a group up toward Big Five Lakes. We had got a late start and it was almost dark before I could start back. I don't like riding at night, but I ride this trail so much I didn't worry about it. So, thinking about how good that beer would taste when I got down, I tethered the horses together and headed down the hill.

'What I didn't know was that my lead horse was night blind. And, at the bend in the trail, at the narrow spot over there, the lead horse walked off into space. But she caught herself and somehow managed to get back up on the trail. I was ahead of her and really couldn't see what happened. Anyway, in her struggle to save herself, she pulled the second horse, Josephine, over the edge. The horse you see down there is Josephine.'"

Dr. James frowned, "My God," he said. "After all this, did you go on to the mine?"

"We had no choice. There was no place to turn around and it would have been a long, long way to walk. So yes, we went on to the mine. And when we got there, the only thing Jeff could tell us about the mine was its name. Said it was named after an Indian chief. Any buildings that might have been there had long since been removed. The mine entry, about eight feet in length, ended in a wall of dynamited rock. There was nothing to see. Just an abandoned wind-swept hole in the ground.

"I did think for a moment or two about what might have happened there, about the hardship of digging for silver at that altitude and bringing in supplies. And I wondered who the miners were and what had happened to them. But for the most part, probably like everyone else, I thought about the ride back down the mountain. I don't know if you've done much climbing, Doc, but going up you're looking at the rock; going down you're looking at how far you might fall.

"So, after a terrifying ride up the mountain to a remote derelict mine, we descend the narrow trail looking into the abyss. And Josephine, the bear, the narrow trail, the river bottom goes with each of us. Everyone fights the urge to get off and walk. We have seen death and resurrection. The scene, the image, the terror—I can still see and feel it to this day."

"How did your kids fare?"

"Sophie was upset, but Sophie's tough. Nate kept his thoughts to himself. I think the experience bound the three of us together, and I think made us all stronger. Certainly closer. Poor Mary, I think, was the most bothered when we later told her what had happened."

"And the happy ending—aside from you sitting here now?"

"I can't tell you about resurrection. But as for the here and now, if like Josephine I die, I will live in Higg. If Higg dies or both of us die, I will have done the noble thing—to have made a gift of myself to someone who has no power. So the story shows I can't lose with this donation, whatever the outcome."

The doctor nodded. "I'd like to think you're right," said Dr. James.

Bart was blowing smoke and he knew it. So, most likely, did the doctor. Bart felt frightened and trapped. He was losing a kidney, and he was losing Birdie. Shaking his head, he stood up, put on his baseball cap, stretched, and checked out the back parking lot.

"It is a great story," Bart said, "And my telling it beat answering your questions for 55 minutes." Bart smiled. Took the doctor's hand. "Wish me luck, Doc. See you when I come down from the mountain."

Ch 41. Understanding

Wednesday

Sophie had wakened early as usual. It would be a few days before she came to terms with Pacific Time. The morning fog had yet to burn off and still rendered a dark image of the outside world. Later the images—the trees, the flowers—would emerge, colored green, yellow, red.

Sophie walked to the kitchen and made some coffee. She usually drank tea but couldn't tolerate the industrial grade stuff her father drank. This morning she wanted to talk with Mrs. Higgins before Bart was up. Once he had "risen"— getting him to live again had started this mess—he would captivate her, and it would be difficult to break away without interrogation. She left him a note. "Dad, I've gone out. Will be back in an hour or so. XOXO, Sophie." With luck, he would not guess where she had gone.

The familiar trail between the two houses was still damp and muddy. A large jumble of tree branches and yard clean-up sat next to the trail and, by its look, had been there awhile. Sophie did not know what she would say. Mrs. Higgins had been a support to both Mom and Dad, helped as Mom struggled with cancer, and looked after Dad after Mom died. How did she view Dad? Did she love him? See him as someone who owed her? Or was he just the source of a body part that would save the life of her husband? She stared at the confusion of branches. Could someone trade the life of one person for another? Could she trade one child for another? Trade Phil for Sarah? No.

And even if the risk weren't as great as she thought, how would this end for her father? The Higgins ride smiling into the sunset? Bart sits alone in his empty house? She needed to know.

Sophie hesitated when she reached the kitchen door. She pulled up the sleeve to her down jacket, looked at her watch. 8:30 am, too early, but so what.

She feared this meeting. Feared finding a person so steely-eyed she would ignore Bart's feelings and possible death to save Higg, a sick old man with a history of cancer.

Mrs. Higgins was in the kitchen, hands covered with flour. She stepped to the sink. "Oh, Sophie, I'm so glad you came over. I missed seeing you the last time you were here. Your dad is so brave and generous. No other person would have offered what he has. I think it's going to turn out well for everyone."

Sophie did not smile. "Bit of a dice roll, wouldn't you say? Russian roulette maybe."

"Oh, I don't think so. The doctors wouldn't perform this procedure if there were any significant risk."

"But we don't really know, do we?"

"Well I know what they tell me. And I do know it's the only chance Higg has. I also know that neither Higg nor I knew of his offer to donate until after your dad made it. I did not ask him to donate and, until he made the offer, I had never talked to him about his making a donation. As to outcome, I've been assured there's nothing beyond the risk from any invasive procedure. Do you know something I don't?

"I think I better just go back before I say something I'd regret."

"Sophie, I didn't ask Bart to donate. Didn't even suggest it. A kidney transplant is no big deal. One night in the hospital and done."

Sophie stared at her. "Sure, except for his medical condition, his injuries from his helicopter crash and his motorcycle accidents. But of course that doesn't matter, does it? Higg gets his kidney and the two of you live happily ever after. And Dad? He gets what, a Christmas card?

Mrs. Higgins took up her baking spoon and began to slowly fold batter. She stared into the bowl for several seconds, then looked Sophie in the face. In a quiet voice she said, "Sophie, no one has said anything about a medical condition or danger to Bart. Both his urologist and his primary doctor approved his donating. They would not allow this procedure if it would endanger Bart. And for that matter, I wouldn't either. Yes, there have been concerns, but with Higg, not with Bart. I don't know anything about motorcycle accidents and helicopter crashes. And I understood you supported your father's donation." She took off her apron. "Let's go talk to your father."

Sophie saw her father as clearly as if he were standing in front of her. You didn't tell her, did you? She was red with anger and wanted to shake him. She was yelling. How could you be so selfish? Do we count for nothing? You die to save someone who may not live even with a transplant?

Mrs. Higgins said, "Sophie, your father's kindness and care has meant the world to me. It gave me comfort when all was black. I would never hurt him. But I know he's doing this for me. Higg and Bart are like oil and water.

"I believe Bart's doctors are correct. If not, I sit in this arid marriage watching the one I care most about sacrifice himself to preserve it. Someone's cruel joke. But I didn't know how you felt. Why don't you and I talk to your father together."

Sophie began to cry. "I've tried everything to talk him out of this. And I know his doctors have approved his donating. I think the problem is mine. I just don't want to lose him."

"And God knows I don't.."

Sophie said, "This was Dad, Dad to the rescue, Dad the good guy. Mrs. Higgins, I'm scared. I don't want him to do this. I hope his doctors are correct." She hugged Mrs. Higgins. They stood there for a moment both crying. "I'm sorry for what I said." She squeezed Mrs. Higgins' hand, turned, and walked out the door.

Ch 42. *Post Op*

Bart skipped the day after his procedure, drugs and anesthesia having obscured his thoughts and reduced his speech to mumbles. On the next day, a nurse appeared, alerted no doubt by some connected machine that translated biology into math. She asked him how he felt. He said he wanted to see Birdie. She told him he must drink water and held a cup for him with a bent straw. Later a doctor came in, dressed in starched blue, obviously important. He prodded, looked under things, asked various questions. Bart asked about Birdie.

Bart dozed. When he woke, the important doctor had gone; a nurse had returned or remained, he couldn't tell. The nurse told him, depending on his condition, he most likely could go home in two or three days. She said his son was waiting to see him.

When Nate appeared, he wore his usual expensive blue sport coat, open collared shirt and grey slacks. He stood for a moment at the foot of Bart's bed until Bart woke. "Hi, Dad," he said. "You look like shit. What have you been doing?"

Bart smiled. "Sex, drugs, rock and roll—well, one out of three. Truthfully, not much. Organ donation is a passive activity. You lie on your back and they do their business on top of you. It's like honeymoon night after you've been married for forty years."

"So where is Birdie?" said Bart. "Not that you're not attractive and witty, but I really had hoped she would be here."

"Well, I think she would have been. I know she intended to. But your best buddy Higg didn't do as well as you. They transported him to UC San Francisco and Birdie went with him. She asked me to come get you. I had nothing to do—I had already emptied the dishwasher—so here I am. I did call Granny T, but she turned me down. Said you hit on her the last time you met."

Bart had half listened after "went with him." Well she is his wife, he thought. She couldn't exactly send him off by his lonesome.

"They tell me you can go home in a day or so if you take it easy. Sophie's coming tomorrow to make sure you keep off the booze and the trampoline. You'll have to avoid the firewater if you don't want the gods tying you to a rock and re-plucking your kidney."

"Not sure about the trampoline," said Bart. "And, as I recall, I think it's my liver that would be in danger."

Nate put his hand on Bart's shoulder. "Your liver's been in danger since you stole your neighbor's fire. Seriously, Dad, take care of yourself. Sophie and I. . . well, we've already lost Mom."

"You're not going to lose me anytime soon. If I thought I was in danger, I wouldn't have done it." Bart looked away from Nate, crossed, then uncrossed his arms. "I am sorry I put you guys through this. I'm sorry about that."

Nate said, "Just behave yourself and get better." He smiled. "The next kidney will be easier."

A nurse came in with "dinner," a compartmentalized plastic tray of unseasoned flora and fauna, much of it with the texture and appeal of wallpaper sizing. Nate opted for the cafeteria, excused himself and left. Said he wanted to try the steak and kidney pie. Bart, who had recovered from his moment of contrition, said "Try the sweetbreads. They're locally sourced."

After dinner, a nurse rechecked fluid sacks and tubes, and gave Bart some pills to help him sleep. He remembered little until waking in severe pain and pushing the call button. In what seemed like two hours later, probably five minutes at most, nurse Rick showed up, unveiled a long plastic tube, and told Bart what he was going to do with it. It hurt. It really hurt, but it felt wonderful to pee.

Sophie arrived that afternoon. She walked into the hospital room and cried when she saw her father. At the same time, she was angry. She told him she loved him, but did not hide her feelings about the operation. On the second night, she sat by his bedside and unloaded. "You didn't even tell us when they scheduled the surgery." Sophie's voice soft, barely above the noise of the hospital.

"And again listen to 1000 reasons why I was making a bad decision."

"You might have changed your mind."

"But I didn't. And all turned out well. I lived. He lived. I wouldn't have donated if I thought I wouldn't live. And the doctors wouldn't have operated if they thought I wouldn't live."

"But there was a chance you might not live."

Bart closed his eyes. Why the argument? The operation was over. Lying on his back, he watched the sweep hand on the wall clock labor toward 12. The rest of the clock did not move.

"Dad?"

"I'm sorry? I tuned out for a second. It seems to be a common occurrence these days."

"I said there was a chance you might not live."

"There's always slight danger with anesthesia, no matter what the age. But even if there were a chance, I still think the decision mine to make. I may value your life, love you as if you were part of me, but once grown, you do the living, make the choices. It's the same with me. And reaching the age of 68, or a hundred for that matter, does not automatically thrust me back into childhood where my progeny parents call the shots."

Sophie said, "We're not on the same sheet of music. I agree people lead their own lives, and to a degree control their own lives. But one person's life affects other people's lives. My birth caused you and Mom to spend money, devote time, develop feelings, care for another human being. Your care of me caused me to love you and trust you. You felt a responsibility toward me and I to you."

She got up and began to walk around, talking down to her father. "I think, as your daughter, as someone who cares and has cared for you, you owed me the courtesy of letting me know when you would undergo surgery. Notice, I'm not challenging your right to donate a kidney, nor your right to lead your own life. No, I'm thinking of feelings, your feelings. I'm thinking of our feelings, the feelings of me and of Nate and the fear of an operation we felt might kill our father. But you didn't think of our feelings. You thought only of Bartholomew Jones."

Hooked-up to monitors and flat on his back, Bart felt trapped while Sophie paced the room. "Sophie, you knew I was going to donate. Why would I drag you 3000 miles to sit in a waiting room?

She did not respond. "Sophie, the doctors would not have performed this operation if there had been any significant risk to me, and I told both of you that before. I know you think the donation stupid, but I think stupid is in the eyes of the donor."

Sophie bowed her head, spread her hands. "OK. Hopefully it all works out the way you wanted. What happens next?"

"Well, we see how Higg responds, and whether the donation makes a difference. It may significantly extend his life. Even if it doesn't, making the donation made a difference to me, and I feel good about it. I couldn't have faced Birdie if I knew I could've saved Higg but chose not to. Maybe she wouldn't have known, but I would have. And I didn't want to live with that. And I believe, if you were me, you would have made the same decision."

"I probably would have, probably would have done the same thing. But Dad, we're your children, your family, and you didn't include us. You left us out. Nate and I are only here because Mrs. Higgins called Nate and told him she couldn't pick you up. What if they were operating on me, and, to save you plane fare, I didn't tell you? Yes, you did the right thing for Higg and for Mrs. Higgins. And you may have done the right thing for yourself. But you left us out. Our feelings did not matter. We were not your clients."

Her comment ended the conversation, and both stopped talking until the silence became uncomfortable.

Bart knew she was right. He had flunked empathy 101 and could hear Dr. James talk about Granny T and Billy and Frank.

"It's OK. I still love you." She leaned over and kissed him on the cheek. "But I want to be your client."

After UC, Higg was transferred to a VA hospital in Phoenix for follow-up treatment. He had had complications and his doctors had questions about his prior cancer. When Higg recovered from the transplant, they would need to test further. In the meantime Higg required continual treatment so Birdie had rented an apartment in Phoenix close to the hospital.

Birdie and Bart spoke often at first. They talked of their feelings, talked of Birdie's return. But Bart soon realized, given Birdie's sense of duty, things would not change as long as Higg lived. He wanted to see her and suggested flying to Phoenix. Birdie had said "No". No good could come of it. And they would not be leaving Phoenix anytime soon. Finally, the calls ended. They changed nothing, served only as a reminder of what could not be. Birdie acted first. "I love you Bart," she had said. "You're the one I always wanted but never had. But these calls tear me up, dangle a life in front of me that I can't have. They're not helping either of us. I think we should say goodbye." Bart agreed. The calls ended. And Bart lived the memories and faced the emptiness of lost love.

Several months later a "For Sale" sign appeared in front of the Higgins house. It's really over thought Bart. He looked at the photos on his desk of Mary, Sophie, his old dog, Molly. In the photo, Mary stands in Yosemite one Spring Day with its falls in full splendor, sunshine showing the mist as diamonds and white. He could smell the mountains, feel the chill in the air. He could see Mary with her changing moods, her laughter. Now Birdie, like Mary, lived only in his head.

Ch 43. Illusion

Parking his big Ford truck behind Dr. James' office felt like homecoming. He opened the door to the smell of sycamore and jasmine, walked to the front of the office and into the discreet one-person waiting room. Craftsman style built-ins mixed with Danish modern furniture and exercise equipment. Out of time, or evidence of progress?

The office door swung open. "Ah", said Dr. James, "the prodigal returns."

Bart rose, gave a slight bow. "Does that mean you're going to pay me?"

"No. It means I welcome your return. Have heard no stories since you left. So I expect one this morning."

They sat in their habitual places, adjacent, not opposed. The office had not changed, and Bart felt comfort in the surroundings—James' blue furniture, James' empty desk, the high windows which sometimes prevented seeing incoming patients.

James got out his notebook and entered the date. In response to the doctor's ritual "How are you feeling?", Bart said things did not turn out as he expected, but turned out as he would have them. Bart told James he would, in fact, tell him a story—a parable, nothing to write home about. He told James if he went over his hour, then it was on the doctor. The doctor agreed and Bart began.

"One chilly morning, before the sun could warm up my office, I met with Martha, the daughter of my long-time clients, Bill and Grace. Bill had died several years back.

"Martha, with stunning good looks, and usually low-key and composed, fought off tears that morning and struggled to talk. She said, 'I don't know how to say this. I don't want to say this. You're going to think I'm crazy.' She opened her purse and took out a tissue, looked around the office as if someone were listening.

"Martha, there's no one here but us," I said, "and no one will know what we talk about today unless you tell them. And I seriously doubt you're crazy." She said nothing, just sat and held herself. I think she was having second thoughts about coming and for a moment I thought she might leave. Finally she took a breath and looked up at me."

"'Jeff and I have been married for 10 years. We have two children. About five years ago, Jeff quit his job at Aerospace. It was a good job, but he wanted his own company. After some research, he started a business selling used telephone equipment—the big stuff used by companies. He sold equipment to foreign businesses and governments, usually South American or African. My parents loaned us the money to start this business—a lot of money. At first all went well, but within several years, you could buy new, better and smaller equipment for much less than the used stuff. The business went under, and we could not repay my parents' loan. In the meantime, to make matters worse, my father had died.

"'A couple of months later, I can't remember exactly, Jeff started going out nights, meeting friends. I felt sorry for him at first, then angry at being left at home with two kids. Sometimes he didn't get home until two or three in the morning. Often he had been drinking. He told me he was exploring a new venture, one that would pay my mother and get us out of debt. In the meantime he asked me to trust him."

"She stopped talking. I thought again she would leave. She said, 'This is so embarrassing. You're going to think I'm losing it. Anyway, Jeff has always taken care of our finances. He pays bills from our on-line account. I have access to this account, but usually don't pay much attention unless I need money for groceries or the children. A couple of weeks ago, I logged into this account and found large deposits from Mom. When I called her, she said things were between me and Jeff. She said Jeff's new venture, at least so far, had worked out well, but I needed to talk to him.'

"'And have you?'

"She shook her head. 'I tried. I couldn't. I was afraid of the answer.' She bit her lip. 'Mr. Jones, I think Jeff's having an affair, having an affair with my mom.'"

"I said, Oh Martha, I'm sure you're wrong. But I must say her worry was not unrealistic. Mother and daughter, both attractive and engaging, could be twins. It was obvious to me that Martha had not talked with her husband. So, I told her to stop the torture and confront Jeff. I said, "No subtlety. He's a male. Ask direct questions.""

"And?" said James.

"And Martha talked to Jeff, asked him straight out, and cried in relief. I imagine Jeff felt about an inch high, felt he had stabbed his love and best friend. But, back to my story. As I said, Jeff's business had gone belly-up, but he had not taken a new job. Unusual, because Jeff had an advanced degree in math and could get hired anywhere. Instead he had talked Grace into another "investment". His new venture was high risk and high reward. He had made a bargain with Grace. If his plan failed, he would get a regular job and keep it until he paid her loans in full. If he succeeded, he would pay her in full and give her a 10% future interest in the venture. The venture succeeded and continues to pay. Jeff didn't tell Martha up front because he knew she would oppose it. Martha still doesn't approve, but they have talked, and things are good on the home front.

"It's like my kidney donation when you think about it. Saved a life. My family opposed my decision; Jeff knew Martha would oppose his. Sometimes, Doc, you just have to say, 'You know, it's my life. I'm going to live it the way I want. And things will not change while I sit here on my behind.'"

"So, speaking of your life, was the kidney donation the

right thing to do?"

Bart wasn't sure. Birdie and Higg now lived in Arizona and their house was up for sale. He had lost contact with Birdie,

"It didn't turn out as I expected.

"So how do you feel about this?"

"I don't feel good about her being gone. And I would have liked at least a thank-you note from Higg, but I understand. When you feel bad, you're not exactly in a thanking mood."

"You think he feels bad?"

"Sure. He got a Christmas present he can't play with."

"You're looking at things from his point of view?"

"Yeah I guess I am. Maybe I've changed."

"What about Birdie, her feelings?"

"I think she feels guilty about her feelings for me, feels she has betrayed Higg. I think she will do the right thing."

"Staying with her husband you mean."

"Yeah. She made a commitment as a wife and will do her duty. But it's more than that. Higg saved her from isolation. He saved her dreams of college, of a life outside rural Minnesota. He gave her her life. It wasn't a love match, but he's always loved her, always been there for here. She will not leave him, and I wouldn't expect her to."

"What about Bart? How's he feeling?"

"I saved a life, and, really when you think about it, I saved a good person—even if he is an engineer."

"If the donation fails?"

"I hope the donation succeeds. If it fails, I may get the girl if Birdie can live with her guilt."

"You've changed."

"Or been exposed."

Dr. James smiled. One last thing: "What does Jeff do?"

Bart was tempted to claim client confidentiality—that he could not ethically disclose what Jeff had done. But he would just be pulling Dr. James' chain. Jeff's current occupation was no secret.

"He plays poker, plays it well. He's paid off Grace's entire loan. And he never slept with Grace or even held her hand for that matter. Shame. Probably would have been worth it."

Ch 44. Aftermath

One Year Later

Amy called at 10:00 am. Said she was bored and might come down to see him. "I think we should go on a cruise together. Get to know each other."

"Works for me, said Bart. "I like the idea of knowing and of stern and bow. I think ships and cabins put them to good use."

"I like those sailing ships with a high mast."

"I think we should take a Carnival cruise to Mexico. One of those three-day things. Then if we don't get along, I can spend the day watching drunk 18-year-olds in string bikinis. "

"Or you could sit on deck and read *The Beautiful and Damned* or *A Day to Remember*. But why would you want to watch 18-year-olds when you could stay in the cabin and drink old wine from a new bottle?"

Bart tapped the phone with his fingers. "Does the port matter?"

"I would hope so," said Amy.

Ah, Amy. Fun, smart, but with a life of her own. Could there be more than an occasional weekend or cruise?

Bart suffered no physical ill effects from his donation, but it had not turned out the way he had imagined. Amy came down from time to time. He had found a new piano teacher and still met with Dr. James, albeit less frequently. Sophie had forgiven him and called weekly to check his progress; Nate had taken up with one of his Ph.D. props. Both children, at least for the present, had given up trying to commit him to a retirement community. Granny T was a year older, and Lily, Bart's faithful standard poodle, still disdained food, but after all these years had yet to starve herself to death. And Bart? Mary had gone, the kids had gone, Birdie and Higg had gone, Amy is more gone than here, Bart is minus a kidney.

Amy having arrived the night before, Bart's biggest problem this morning was a small hangover and an urgent need for coffee. He walked into the kitchen, made coffee and returned to the living room to gather empty wine glasses and discarded clothing. During the evening, Amy had talked of her life, her career and her travels. Told Bart she had agreed to supervise a graduate program on Corfu for six months and would be leaving in several weeks. Asked Bart to join her.

Bart liked the idea but not the short notice. He worried about Lily.

Looking out the kitchen window, Bart saw someone had removed the Higgins' "For Sale" sign. Granny T had told him she thought they had sold the house, said they had had several offers.

It was hard to look at the Higgins' house with its memories. It seemed like a past life. Apple pies smelling of cinnamon, Birdie sitting in Bart's kitchen, the dying Higg. Bart remembered her kindness and her struggle. They had had but one night together.

Amy presented no such challenge as she emerged from the bedroom wearing not much of anything and poured herself a cup of coffee.

Bart said, "You're going to freeze to death. I'll get you a robe."

"Or" she said, "we could go back to bed."

"Thought you had to be in San Francisco by 3:00."

"Oh, yes, I do, and it's important." Disappointed, she shook her head. "Come to Larkspur. Come to Corfu."

"I'll get you a robe."

Amy clothed, Bart walked outside and picked up the Wall Street Journal and the San Sebastian Morning News. The WSJ told Bart national and international news, San Sebastian news of local import. As usual, Bart scanned the obits first and smiled when he didn't see his name. He hadn't known most of these people, but he had known one and read the obituary with care.

"Martin Higgins, formerly of San Sebastian, died April 1 after a protracted

illness. Mr. Higgins, a long-time resident of San Sebastian, served as president

of Higgins and Associates, Civil Engineers until his retirement in 2015. Mr.

Higgins is survived by his wife, Birdie V. Higgins. In lieu of flowers, donations

may be sent . . ."

Bart folded the paper and put it aside. He would not live again in Higg, though some day he might share Higg's feelings.

Amy emerged from the bedroom, dressed and ready for travel. "I'm going to be gone for six months. I don't want to leave. I feel like it's college all over again. Think about coming with me or joining me in a month or so."

"I've thought about it since you first brought it up." Bart carried her overnight bag to her car, hugged her, said, "Call me when you get home. We can talk about arrangements."

As she drove off, Bart still remembered her leaving 40 years earlier. "Leaving" was the story of his life: first Amy, then Mary, then Birdie, then Amy again. Dreaming of Amy and of Corfu, he walked back into the house, turned on his computer, and settled in his big office chair. He didn't like the idea of boarding Lily for six months, but this time Lily might have to suffer. Six months on a Greek isle with Amy? He wanted to go. Maybe he could take Lily with him.

Lily meanwhile erupted in barking and raced to the front door. God, what now? Granny T with another petition? Amy forget something? He combed his hair with his hands and opened the door.

"Hi Bart," said Birdie.

———————

ABOUT THE AUTHOR

Jk George

A retired lawyer, JK George lives with his wife of 58 years, his dog, Lily, and his wife's evil cat, Max. The family divides their time between two small communities, one on the Central California Coast, the other in the Sierra Nevada Mountains. A graduate of Stanford University, George received his certificate in novel writing from Stanford Continuing Studies in 2022. The Evening of Bartholomew Jones is his first novel.

Made in United States
Troutdale, OR
12/12/2023

15781760R00130